"We need to ta
want to make

Clay reached out to cup her cheek in the palm of his hand, his thumb brushing across her lips, her soft, smooth cheek. Her gaze never wavered. What he saw in her eyes almost leveled him. She kissed the pad of his thumb, her eyes filled with a need that mirrored his own.

He swept Josie up into his arms and carried her up the stairs to the bedroom, all reason and logic and suspicion discarded as quickly as he planned to discard their clothing. He wanted her. And he planned to have her. Right now. Later he'd deal with whatever she had to tell him.

She sensed his body heat draw her to him. The masculine scent of him mixed with the smell of leather and horses. Intoxicating. Her body felt alive, everything magnified as if this were the first time....

He was close. Too close. To her. To the truth.

Dear Harlequin Intrigue Reader,

The thrills never stop at Harlequin Intrigue. This month, get geared up for danger and desire in double helpings!

There's something about a mysterious man that makes him all the more appealing. In *The Silent Witness* (#565), Alex Coughlin is just such a man on assignment and undercover. But can he conceal his true feelings for Nicki Michaels long enough to catch a killer? Join Dani Sinclair and find out as she returns to FOOLS POINT.

The search for the truth is Clay Jackson's only focus—until he learns the woman he never stopped loving was keeping the biggest secret of all...a baby. See why *Intimate Secrets* (#566) are the deepest with author B.J. Daniels.

Patricia Rosemoor winds up her SONS OF SILVER SPRINGS miniseries this month. Reed is the last Quarrels brother to go the way of the altar as he enters a marriage of convenience with the one woman he thought he'd never have, in *A Rancher's Vow* (#567).

Finally, welcome multitalented author Jo Leigh as she contributes her first Harlequin Intrigue title, *Little Girl Found* (#568). She also begins a three-month bonanza of books! Look for her titles from Harlequin American Romance (June) and Harlequin Temptation (July). You won't be sorry.

Gripping tales of mystery, suspense that never lets up and sizzling romance to boot. Pick up all four titles for the total Harlequin Intrigue experience.

Sincerely,

Denise O'Sullivan
Associate Senior Editor
Harlequin Intrigue

Intimate Secrets
B.J. Daniels

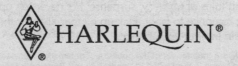

HARLEQUIN®

TORONTO • NEW YORK • LONDON
AMSTERDAM • PARIS • SYDNEY • HAMBURG
STOCKHOLM • ATHENS • TOKYO • MILAN • MADRID
PRAGUE • WARSAW • BUDAPEST • AUCKLAND

This one's for LuAnn Rod, who shared her love of horses with me, and shares my love of snowboarding. See you on the slopes, girlfriend!

ISBN 0-373-22566-0

INTIMATE SECRETS

Copyright © 2000 by Barbara Heinlein

Visit us at www.eHarlequin.com

Printed in U.S.A.

ABOUT THE AUTHOR

Born in Houston, B.J. Daniels is a former Southern girl who grew up on the smell of gulf sea air and Southern cooking. But like her characters, her home is now in Montana, not far from Big Sky, where she snowboards in the winters and boats in the summers with her husband and daughters. She does miss gumbo and Texas Barbecue, though! Her first Harlequin Intrigue novel was nominated for the *Romantic Times* Reviewer's Choice Award for best first book and best Harlequin Intrigue. She is a member of Romance Writers of America, Heart of Montana and Bozeman Writers Group. B.J. loves to hear from readers. Write to her at: P.O. Box 183, Bozeman, MT 59771.

Books by B.J. Daniels

HARLEQUIN INTRIGUE

312—ODD MAN OUT
353—OUTLAWED!
417—HOTSHOT P.I.
446—UNDERCOVER CHRISTMAS
493—A FATHER FOR HER BABY
533—STOLEN MOMENTS
555—LOVE AT FIRST SIGHT
566—INTIMATE SECRETS

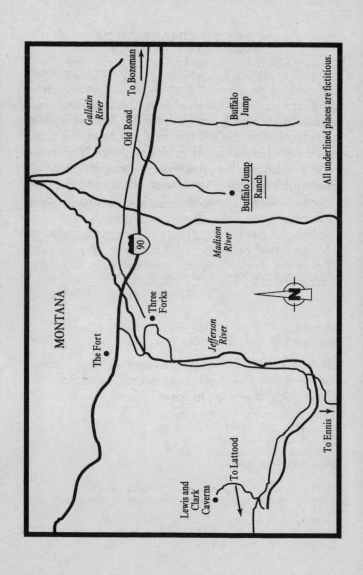

MONTANA

Gallatin River

To Bozeman

Old Road

Buffalo Jump

Buffalo Jump Ranch

90

Madison River

The Fort

Three Forks

N

Jefferson River

Lewis and Clark Caverns

To Lattood

To Ennis

All underlined places are fictitious.

CAST OF CHARACTERS

Josie O'Malley — When her secret past comes looking for her, it brings the two men she fears most back into her life.

Clay Jackson — He's chased a thief all the way from Texas to Montana in search of priceless jewels. But what he finds is more precious than any jewel.

Ivy O'Malley — She's the spitting image of her mother — except she's got her daddy's eyes.

Raymond Degas — He disappeared two years ago. Why has he resurfaced now of all times?

Odell Burton — He swore revenge — even from the grave.

Mildred Andrews — The elderly woman would do anything to protect the baby left in her care. But would it be enough?

Brandon Williams — He just wanted his jewels back.

Ruth Slocum — The tough old ranch woman passed on what she'd learned about horses — and men — to Josie. Now it was up to Josie.

Dear Reader,

I've always loved caves. Although I'm claustrophobic, I can't resist them, especially Lewis and Clark Caverns near Three Forks, Montana. I'm fascinated by this underground dark world, so hidden, so beautiful, so elusive.

Caves, and my fascination with secrets and the way they have of coming back to haunt you, provided the spark for *Intimate Secrets*.

Something is waiting in the darkness. Come on down. If you dare.

B. J. Daniels

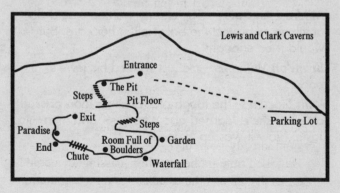

Prologue

He looked like the rest of the tourists as he bought a ticket at the small booth on the mountainside. The next tour started in ten minutes. It would be the last tour of the day.

Perfect.

The rays of the sinking sun slanted across the top of the mountain, painting the buildings with bronzed heat. Below, the Jefferson River snaked emerald green through the rocky canyon. On the mountainside, the sagebrush stood dusty gray in a ground already gone dry.

He killed time in the gift shop, passing up a cold beer, ice cream and the usual curios for a schematic of the caverns. With five minutes to spare, he went back to wait by the ticket booth, anxious. Anxious to get deep in the cool darkness of the caves. Anxious to confront an old enemy he knew would be waiting down there for him. But mostly, anxious to find the one thing he needed, the perfect hiding place.

He'd been bowled over when he'd seen the sign just outside of Three Forks, Montana. Lewis and Clark Caverns 15 Miles. It had been more than fate or good fortune. It had been divine intervention.

A young guide called his tour group, explaining they would have to hike up to the cave entrance. There used to be a small train, but now visitors had to walk. He didn't mind walking the half mile, even uphill along the paved trail, a trail easy enough for his grandmother.

Once inside, there was a two-mile trek and a three-hundred-foot descent, into the bowels of the cave, ending with six hundred rock-carved stairs to the exit.

Perfect.

He quickly got ahead of everyone else, anxious to get inside the mountain. But he also liked the view down the steep mountainside and wondered how many tourists had fallen. Sweat broke out under his arms, ran down his sides.

But it wasn't from exertion. It was pure expectation. He *hated* confined places. Hated anything that reminded him of the root cellar back at his grandmother's farm. The dark, cool, raw earth. The musty, wet-smelling air. The darkness pressing against him, squeezing the life from him. The taste and smell and feel of fear.

Claustrophobia. It was his only failing. But also the only thing that still aroused him to the point of rapture. The ultimate. The little death. It gave him an edge other people didn't have. Would never understand.

He couldn't wait to get inside. He couldn't wait to find exactly what he was looking for. A hole. Something small enough he would have to squeeze through. A space beyond the hole, far enough off the tour route that no one could find him. A place where he could finish what he'd started.

At the top, he had to wait for the rest of the group. He tried not to be impatient as he stood at the mouth of the entrance and gazed down into the confining darkness. Soon, he thought, soon.

The tour guide led the group through the caverns, pointing out stalactites and stalagmites, flowstone and dripstone. He paid little attention. He knew all about caves. He did listen, though, when the guide spoke about one of the first explorers getting lost, losing his candle and spending three days in the dark, unable to move. The man had been temporarily blind and completely disoriented from the days in total blackness.

More than five hundred feet into the cave, he found what he was looking for. The perfect place to disappear into the blinding darkness.

He hung back in the small room, pretending to admire the iciclelike lime deposits, wondering if the tour guide would miss him. He doubted it, out of a group of more than a dozen. They were all more interested in the rock formations than some nondescript tourist.

The group began to move on. He waited behind a large stalagmite. "Do we have everyone?" the tour guide inquired. No one said anything and the light diminished as the tour moved on, leaving him alone in the dark.

He waited, standing in the dizzying darkness, his face frozen in fear. He loved this part the best. The absolute blackness. The chilling silence. The disorientation that set in within seconds. He thought of the explorer down here without his candle. Trapped. Unable to see anything. Unable to move. And no one to hear his cries for help.

When he couldn't take another second of it, he snapped on the tiny flashlight he'd brought and shone it into the hole he'd found. Small. Just enough room to barely get through. He got down on his hands and knees, then his belly, and taking a ragged breath, wriggled into the narrow tunnel.

He slithered like a snake, deeper and deeper into the confined cavity, squirming around the tight blind corners. Five minutes in, the tunnel ended in a solid rock wall.

He froze. He couldn't go on any farther. Nor could he turn around. This would do just fine. The perfect place to hide a small child.

He started to back out, but his body stuck, now suddenly too large for the cramped rock channel he'd wormed through. Instantly, sweat cloaked his already-clammy body. The constant fifty-degree air raised goose bumps, chilling him. He fought for each breath, but let the panic come, the euphoria of fear.

He tried backing out again. If he'd come through it, he could get out, right? Except he'd come through headfirst, and since there wasn't enough room to turn around, he had no choice but to go out feet first. Feet first like a corpse.

Prostrate, he dug in with his toes, inching backward, squeezing through the tight, constricting passage, the claustrophobia taunting him: "You'll never get out. The rocks are compressing, the hole contracting, the mountain closing in on you."

His mouth went dry as dust. He gasped for breath, his heart lunging in his chest. Minutes ticked off like hours. The tiny flashlight banged against a rock, dimmed, almost went out.

He was breathing hard now, but the air seemed too thin. Maybe he'd made a wrong turn. But he knew better. He struggled for each breath, each inch backward, the hole now endless as eternity. Or hell. His hell.

Then suddenly his toes lost purchase. Nothing but air. Air and space. He shoved himself back-

ward with his hands and slipped through the opening, scrambling out of the hole.

Free.

For a few more desperate moments, he stood in
the room where the tour group had left him behind,
shining the light across the ghostly rock formations, forcing back the claustrophobia the way he
forced back the dark.

He didn't have much time. He gripped the flashlight, suddenly afraid he might drop it. That he
might be the one who ended up trapped down here
in the deafening darkness.

The irony amused him as much as the bitter taste
of his own fear. He stood, just long enough to
catch his breath, then hurriedly wound his way
through the cold cavity until he was within earshot
of the tour group, the worn trail easy to follow. He
waited until the guide moved on to the next item
of interest before he caught up and fell in with the
others.

Then it was over. One last rock-carved wide tunnel and he was back outside again, more than three
hundred feet below the entrance, walking down another paved path, smiling smugly, feeling trium-
phant.

But the euphoria never lasted long.

Fortunately, he'd be back. For the cave's dark,
confined allure. For a well-deserved ending to the
two years he'd lost. He'd make up for it. In spades.

Once he'd snatched the kid, he'd finally get what was rightfully his.

He chuckled to himself as he looked across the mountainside toward Three Forks, Montana. Wouldn't Josie O'Malley be surprised when she saw him. Soon, Josie. Real soon.

Chapter One

Josie reined in her horse and looked out at the valley that ran spring green to the still-snowcapped mountain peaks.

"Look at that, Ivy," she whispered as she hugged the toddler in front of her, resting her chin on top of her daughter's blond head. "Isn't it pretty?"

The sun slipped behind the mountains, turning the Montana sky a brilliant orange that radiated across the horizon, making the last of the day glow as warm and bright as any Josie had ever seen.

"Pwetty," her fourteen-month-old repeated.

Ivy's hair still had that baby smell, the loose curls a pale blond and down-soft, so much like Josie's own. Ivy looked just as Josie had at that age. Except for her eyes. Instead of being the color of bluebonnets, they were a startling deep, dark brown—just like the baby's father's.

Because of that, Josie never looked at her daughter without being reminded of him—and Texas. Each brought an ache of its own.

As beautiful as Montana was, it wasn't Texas. This time of year, the Texas hill country would be alive with bluebonnets and Indian paintbrush against a backdrop of live oak. The air would be scented with cedar.

So different from Montana. She stared out at the lush landscape and breathed in the sweet scent of pine. The Buffalo Jump Ranch, surrounded by snowy peaks, towering pines and rocky bluffs, was thousands of miles from Texas—and the past.

But more important, she'd found what she wanted to do with her life here in Montana. For the first time, Josie O'Malley felt truly at peace.

The realization startled her. She'd always felt at odds with the diminutive flaxen-haired sprite with the bright blue eyes she saw staring back at her from the mirror. They said she looked like her mother, but her father and brothers assured her she was nothing like sweet-tempered, soft-spoken Katherine Donovan O'Malley had been.

Instead, Josie had a wild spirit, as wild as the Texas land she'd grown up in, with a rebellious temperament her father said came from her namesake, her great-grandmother Josephine O'Malley.

Josie didn't mind the comparison to her great-grandmother, who'd been a Wild West rodeo trick rider. In fact, Josie had clung to her rebellious spirit when her father and older brothers had tried to break it the same way they broke their horses— by trying to break her will. In the end, they'd only succeeded in driving her away.

As she hugged her daughter in the fading light, Josie realized with more than a little surprise how far she'd come—and not in miles. For the first time, she really *did* feel…ready. Maybe now she could do what she'd sworn on her great-grandmother's memory she would do.

The horse nickered softly beneath them, his ears coming up as he raised his head and sniffed the warm breeze. Suddenly his ears lay back as if he saw something in the trees.

Josie tensed as well, her gaze going past the aspens to the dark edge of pines that bordered the horse ranch to the north. The first shadows of evening had settled in the trees, but she was close enough that she could see him. A man. Standing not fifty feet away. Looking right at her. Watching her and Ivy.

Startled, Josie jerked the reins, making the horse jump to the side, making her lose sight of the man as she held Ivy to her. She steadied the horse, upset with herself for treating the mare with such roughness, and focused again on the pines.

An icy shaft of fear sliced through her, bone-deep, as she stared into the shadows, frantically searching for the man she'd seen. A man she'd recognized.

But no one looked back at her from the shadowed darkness of the trees. Nothing moved. Not the thick, dark branches of the pines. Not the silver-sided, coinlike leaves of the aspens. Certainly not the man she'd thought she'd seen standing there, watching her and Ivy.

The sun slipped behind the mountains, shadows deepening. Suddenly the day no longer felt warm. Or safe.

Josie reined the horse around and, hugging her daughter to her, rode toward the small cabin that had become her home, afraid to look back. At the pines. Or the past.

Afraid to acknowledge who she'd thought she'd glimpsed watching her from the shelter of the trees.

A man who'd been dead for more than two years.

JOSIE WOKE WITH A START, jerking upright, heart pounding, her gaze at once darting to the crib in the bedroom across the hall.

Sun streamed in the window, blinding her. The crib appeared empty. In that instant, the memory of the man she'd seen yesterday in the trees came back, as dark and ominous as an omen.

Then she heard Ivy's sweet laughter. Eyes adjusting to the sunlight, Josie saw her daughter standing in the crib, trying to catch dust motes in her chubby little hands.

Just the sight of Ivy filled her with a wave of relief that threatened to drown her. She got up quickly and took her daughter in her arms, needing to hold her, to assure herself that Ivy was safe.

But the initial fear she'd felt on waking receded slowly, the memory of the man in the pines too fresh. Too real.

Odell Burton was dead. And Josie O'Malley didn't believe in ghosts. But just thinking she'd seen him had shaken her more than she wanted to admit. Especially since at that moment she'd been feeling safe.

As she and Ivy ate oatmeal on the porch in the morning sun, she tried to get back that feeling of peace, however brief, she'd felt the day before. Logically, she knew she'd seen a man—just not Odell.

But the memory of the man watching her and Ivy from the trees still clung to her like the remnants of a bad dream. Something about him had scared her. And Josie prided herself on not scaring easily.

The last time she saw Odell had been on her family's ranch in Texas. She'd turned to find him watching her and realized he'd just come out of the barn. He had an odd expression on his face. He looked almost nervous.

That wasn't like him. She'd known him since they were kids. His father raised rough stock for rodeos down the road from the O'Malley Ranch.

But there had always been something about him— She shivered. His interest in her had always unnerved her. Even when they were kids. Worse, when they were older and he'd realized she wasn't interested in him. Odell had a hard time accepting no. It was probably one of the reasons he'd gotten in trouble with the law at such an early age.

She fed Ivy a few bites of oatmeal, then relinquished the baby spoon, although Ivy was getting more oatmeal on her face than in her mouth.

Josie knew that even thinking she'd seen Odell was some kind of subconscious reminder of everything she still feared from two years ago. She and Ivy were safe. But obviously, her subconscious didn't believe it.

Maybe it was because she'd been thinking about going home to Texas. Just the thought of going home filled her with excitement—and anxiety. It had been two years. She'd broken all ties with her family when she'd taken off the way she had. Not that it could have been helped under the circumstances. Still, she wished things had been different.

Going home meant facing more than Odell's ghost. More than her father and brothers. She couldn't be sure what kind of reception she'd get at the O'Malley Ranch. But at least she knew what to expect from Clay Jackson.

Clay. She closed her eyes for a moment, unconsciously smiling at a distant memory. Clay had grown up on the adjacent ranch, the Valle Verde. He'd been her brother Dustin's age. Six years older, the boys had seen her only as a kid—and a girl at that.

But Clay was always kind to her, and from the time she could remember she'd had a crush on him. When he went away to college, she dreamed of the day he'd return home to the ranch—and her. She knew that once he saw her all grown-up he'd fall for her, just as she'd fallen for him so many years before.

Unfortunately, she thought, her smile fading, he hadn't come back. He'd fallen in love with a woman named Maria and he'd become a deputy sheriff, and he appeared to have no intention of ever returning to ranching.

Then one day he'd just reappeared. She'd looked up and there he was framed against the Texas sky, his broad shoulders blocking out the sun.

Except it wasn't exactly as she'd dreamed. She heard through the ranch rumor mill that the woman he'd fallen in love with after college had run off with someone else, Clay had turned in his badge, and being the youngest, he'd come home to take over the ranch so his father could retire.

He'd just turned thirty. Josie, twenty-four.

Prize-winning horses and Clay, right next door. Unfortunately, she hadn't known then that he'd brought more than just a fine string of horses to the Valle Verde. He'd brought the bitterness of a man who'd lost the woman he'd loved and had sworn never to love again.

She opened her eyes now, all the old regret coming back. She'd naively believed she could heal his broken heart, if Clay would give her the chance. If he'd see her as a woman—and not the tomboy she'd been. He'd once told her she was the wildest thing east of the Pecos, wilder than an "unbroke" stallion.

She hired on in his stables, mucking out the stalls, although she had a degree in ranch management. It wasn't until later that she'd found out Clay had only hired her as a favor to her family. It seemed Clay arrogantly believed he was the man who could handle her. That he would be the one to tame her wild spirit as a favor to her father and brothers.

How wrong he'd been. In the end, he'd only succeeded in spurring her to live up to his expectations—and her foolishness had ultimately cost her dearly.

Clay Jackson had never seen her as anything more than Dustin's wild kid sister. She doubted that would change when they saw each other again.

She looked over at her daughter, who was now banging the high-chair tray with her spoon and dropping globs of oatmeal to the floor with her other hand.

One thing was certain. She was *ready* to go home to Texas. But did she dare?

She turned at the sound of a car coming up the road. "Here comes Millie," she told her daughter.

Ivy stopped banging her tray to look out the porch screen at the approaching car. "Miwillie!" she cried, all smiles.

Josie lifted her daughter from the high chair and wiped her face, kissing the wriggling, giggling toddler's damp, clean cheek when she'd finished.

"Mornin'," Mildred Andrews called as she joined them on the porch. Mildred was short and squat, a small gray-haired woman in her early sixties with a pleasant round face and an ever-present cheerfulness. She made Ivy laugh. She made Josie smile. There was something so homespun about the grandmotherly woman. And best of all, she loved children—especially Ivy. They'd hit it off immediately, and Josie felt secure knowing Mildred was caring for her daughter. She was the grandmother Ivy would never have.

"I thought I'd take Ivy into the big city," Mildred was saying. The big city Millie referred to was the tiny town of Three Forks, Montana, named for the Jefferson, Madison and Gallatin rivers that joined outside of town to make the Missouri River. "Can I get you anything from the grocery store?"

Josie scribbled down a quick list, the heavy weight of anxiety lightening at just the sight of Mildred. Ivy let out squeals of delight as the older woman took the list and Ivy out to the car. Ivy loved to go "bye-bye."

It wasn't until later, standing on the porch, watching Mildred pull away, Ivy waving and throwing wet kisses from the car seat in the back, that Josie felt a stab of doubt, like a thin blade of ice piercing her heart. She told herself she had nothing to worry about. Ivy was in good hands with Mildred. But she knew that wasn't what worried her. Dead or not, Odell Burton and the past were still haunting her.

SHE HEADED FOR THE STABLES, knowing work would be the only thing that could get her mind off her worries.

By early afternoon, she was feeling better and relieved to see Mildred's car coming up the dirt road in a cloud of dust. Ivy's cherub-cheeked face peered out from the back seat.

Josie walked up the hillside to the cabin where she and Ivy lived, a rustic two-story log structure with a screened-in porch off the front and a deck and stairs off the back of the second story.

From the porch, Josie could see not only the

stables and main ranch house, but beyond, across the valley and the Madison River, to the tops of the grain elevators in town.

But the view from the second-story deck off the back was her favorite. She often stood there, looking over the pines to the pale yellow band of sandstone known as the Madison Buffalo Jump. For years, before the Native Americans had horses, the site was used to harvest buffalo on foot.

Josie couldn't imagine a time when buffalo roamed this river valley. She especially couldn't imagine a time before horses. She'd had a horse since birth and had been riding almost as long. She loved horses and understood them in a way she'd never understood men.

Ivy was already out of the car and headed up the steps by the time Josie reached the cabin. She stopped at the car to help Mildred carry in the groceries. A widow, Mildred often stayed over. They'd fallen into the habit of having dinner together, with Mildred surprising them with her favorite dishes.

"Your daughter causes a commotion everywhere she goes," Mildred said, laughing as she lowered a bag of groceries to the table.

"A commotion?" Josie asked, eyeing Ivy as she let the screen door slam behind her.

The cabin was narrow, built tall rather than wide. It ran shotgun style from living room to kitchen with a set of open stairs on the left up to the second-floor bath and two bedrooms.

Josie heard Ivy let out a squeal as she took off across the living room after Millie.

"What did Ivy get into now?" Josie asked with a pretend groan as she set down her armful of groceries, then turned to grab her daughter as she toddled past. She scooped Ivy into her arms and hugged her tightly. She couldn't seem to hug her enough. Everything about the child filled her with awe. Josie never knew she could feel like this. It was the second revelation in her life.

"She was an absolute angel!" Mildred said in Ivy's defense. "It's not her fault that she's so adorable that even good-looking, smooth-talking cowboys can't resist her."

"Good-looking cowboys?" Josie asked, feeling the first prickle of unease as she put the wriggling Ivy back down.

"Even at the store," Mildred continued as she began putting Josie's groceries away. "He just couldn't take his eyes off her. He finally had to come over and say hello."

Josie felt a wave of anxiety flood her.

Mildred looked up and saw her reaction. "Oh, it wasn't like that. He was perfectly adorable. Polite with an accent like yours."

Josie felt the floor buckle under her. Blood

drained from her head. Her ears rang. "A Texas accent?"

Mildred looked scared, too, now. She'd paled, her fingers nervously kneading the edges of a box of macaroni and cheese.

Josie could barely form the words. "What did he look like?"

"Oh, Josie, I didn't really pay him much mind," she cried. "He was just a nice-looking cowboy in jeans, boots and a Stetson. I guess he was tall and dark and—" She realized what she was saying. "—and yes, as corny as it sounds, handsome. But he didn't do or say anything...inappropriate, and with tourists coming through town all the time—"

"What did he do and say?" Josie asked, trying to keep the fear out of her voice. Trying not to scare Mildred any more than she already had.

"He said something like 'Oh, what a beautiful little girl.' Ivy was giggling. She liked him. Then he said, 'She looks just like someone I used to know. The spitting image. Except for the eyes.' Something like that."

A chill raced up her spine like a Montana blizzard blowing in. She tried to tell herself it was nothing. Just like thinking she saw Odell in the pines yesterday.

This had only been a cowboy in a grocery store. Ivy always attracted attention with that pale blond hair of hers and her angelic face. And those startling dark eyes. So why did Josie find herself shaking, fear making her heart pound and her knees weak with worry?

She saw Mildred frown as if she'd remembered something that disturbed her. "What is it?"

"He *did* ask her name. I didn't think it would hurt anything."

Josie found breath to ask. "You told him her name was Ivy O'Malley?"

Mildred quickly shook her head. "I just told him her name was Ivy."

Josie tried to breathe. She'd kept her name when she'd left Texas. She'd wanted something of her family to take with her, something to give her child, and after Odell's death, she'd believed that no one would ever come looking for her.

But now she realized keeping her name had been a silly, sentimental and very foolish thing to do. If someone from Texas *was* looking for her, she'd made it easy. So didn't that mean if the man *had* been looking for her, he'd have already found her? He wouldn't be watching her from a stand of trees. Or chasing after Ivy in some grocery store.

"I'm sure it was nothing," she said, trying to reassure Mildred. Trying even harder to reassure herself.

Mildred looked more worried. "Do you think you might know him?"

That was the question, wasn't it? Tall, dark and

handsome definitely ruled out her brothers. They were tall, handsome and quite the ladies' men with their Irish charm, but they were blond like her.

Unfortunately, tall, dark and handsome *did* fit both Odell Burton and Clay Jackson. But Odell was dead. And Clay… Well, he didn't know where she was and didn't have any reason to come looking for her. At least not one he knew about.

Don't panic. Mildred's right. It all sounds innocent enough. So what if he had a Texas accent? Texas is a big state. So what if he took an interest in Ivy?

But Josie knew what she really feared. That the man was somehow connected to Odell Burton and what had happened in Texas two years ago.

"Did you happen to see what he was driving?" Josie asked.

Mildred shook her head. "Did I do something wrong?"

"No," she assured the older woman. "It might be someone I know from Texas. You see, no one back home knows where I am. I left in a hurry." She smiled at Mildred. "I found myself pregnant and knew if I stuck around, my father would either demand a shotgun wedding or shoot the man. The truth is, he'd have probably shot him." How could she explain the Texas law of the West when it came to daughters? Or for that matter, Texas cowboys and their codes of honor?

"It's none of my business," Mildred said. "I didn't mean to pry—"

"I want to tell you," she said. Mildred needed to know the truth—well at least some of it—to keep Ivy safe. "I didn't want anyone to know about Ivy or who her father was. He was the last thing Ivy and I needed."

"I'm sorry to hear that," Mildred said. "Then you think this man I saw might be looking for you?"

"I don't know," she admitted. But she intended to find out. If the man was still in town. "Would you mind watching Ivy for a little while tonight?"

Mildred readily agreed. "He really did seem like such a nice man."

THERE WEREN'T MANY PLACES to stay in a town the size of Three Forks, Montana. As Josie left in one of the old ranch trucks, instead of her own truck with Texas plates, she was thinking about where the cowboy stranger with the Texas accent might be staying.

She figured it wouldn't take much to find him— if he was still around. There was the Sacajawea Inn, a white, wood-framed historic hotel on the north edge of town. Or several motels.

She decided to start with the Broken Spur on the south end of town, but a block before the motel, she spotted a newer black Dodge pickup parked on a side street with the silhouette of a cowboy behind the wheel and Texas plates.

Distracted, she barely missed hitting an older model Lincoln Continental that sped out of the Broken Spur motel parking lot and pulled in front of her, headed for Main Street.

Her heart was still pounding over her close call when a set of bright headlights filled her cab. She looked in her rearview mirror to see that the Dodge pickup with the Texas plates had pulled out and fallen in behind her.

Flipping up her rearview mirror, she pulled her western hat down and stayed low in her seat, telling herself the truck wasn't following her. Anyone going into town would come this way. It was a coincidence that the truck had pulled out behind her at that moment. Right.

She tried not to look back as she turned left onto Main Street. Downtown Three Forks was only about four blocks long. She went two of those blocks and parked diagonally between two cars in front of the Headwaters Café, the most well-lit part of town and the busiest this time of night.

Immediately she realized that if she got out, she'd be caught in the pickup's headlights like a deer on the highway. She shut off her engine and slid down in the seat, knowing no matter what she did, if the pickup *was* following her, the driver knew where to find her.

Facing the inescapable, she watched the pickup park back up the street a few spaces away. She could see the driver silhouetted behind the wheel, a man wearing a cowboy hat, his face shaded and dark. But she could tell he was looking her way. Her heart lurched, her pulse taking off at a sprint as he opened his pickup door and stepped out.

It had been two years since she'd last seen the tall, broad-shouldered cowboy, but there was no mistaking him or the impact he had on her.

He pushed back his Stetson and glanced in her direction as he walked toward her truck. Her breath caught in her throat. What was Clay Jackson doing in Montana?

Chapter Two

Josie held her breath as Clay started in her direction, her heart pounding. He stepped up onto the sidewalk, the heels of his expensive boots tapping lightly as he walked. He wore a gray Stetson, a western-cut leather coat and jeans. He looked like he belonged here. Or maybe Clay just had a way of looking like he belonged anywhere.

As he neared her truck, she slid farther down in the seat, afraid it would do no good. Of course he'd seen her. He'd been following her! He'd watched her park. He'd know that she hadn't had time to get out of the truck.

She grimaced, realizing she was caught. She waited for him to turn at her front left fender and walk back to her door, maybe tap on the window, or knowing Clay, just stand waiting until she acknowledged his presence.

To her amazement, he didn't slow in front of her truck, didn't come alongside. Instead, he walked to the café entrance, his gaze not on her or the ranch truck at all, but down the street, toward the Town Club bar, where the rusted, dented cream-colored Lincoln Continental that she'd almost hit a few minutes earlier was now parked.

In fact, it was as if he hadn't seen her at all slumped down in the seat, peeking out from under the brim of her hat.

It suddenly hit her. Clay Jackson hadn't been following her! Wasn't looking for her!

She felt a bubble of relieved laughter float up. As far as she could tell he didn't even know she was here in Three Forks.

But if he wasn't looking for her, then what was he doing here?

She watched with interest as he entered the Headwaters Café, took a seat at a front table. He looked out the large picture window in the direction of the Lincoln as a waitress slid a cup of coffee in front of him. The Lincoln hadn't moved, but the driver, Josie noticed, was no longer inside.

She studied Clay, thinking how little he'd changed, as if life had stood still back in Texas, back on his Valle Verde Ranch. While time had flown for her and everything had changed—especially her. And yet just the sight of him still evoked a mix of emotions, regret at the top of the list and an even stronger emotion that she'd spent two years trying to forget.

She rolled down her window and let the cool air rush in, feeling the flush of memory play in her mind like a country-western song, making her ache with a longing of something unfulfilled. An odd feeling, considering the way things had ended.

She forced another memory to the surface, one that firmly put her feet back on the ground and cleared her head of all romantic notions about him. The day Clay Jackson had forbidden her to go near his prized horses other than to clean out their stalls.

But as she watched him now, she knew her problems with Clay ran a lot deeper than his horses. Or her unresolved feelings for him.

She studied him, wondering what he could be doing here. She doubted horses had brought him all the way to Montana.

As she watched him idly sip his coffee, she realized she wasn't going to find out. He wasn't looking for her. Wasn't that enough? She started the truck and backed out, hoping he wouldn't notice her. It hadn't been that long ago she'd wanted more than anything for Clay to notice her. To see her not as Shawn O'Malley's wild daughter but as the woman she'd become.

Funny how times had changed.

Keeping her face turned away, she drove away from the café—and Clay—down to the end of the street and doubled back, taking side streets until she was clear of town.

She told herself that the man Mildred had seen at the grocery store had to have been Clay. But he wouldn't have recognized Ivy as being Josie's. Or guessed who the father was. He had more pressing concerns than a fourteen-month-old toddler with pale blond hair and dark eyes. Or that baby's mother. But just in case, Josie would stay close to the ranch and keep Ivy close as well.

She peeked in on Ivy when she reached the cabin, only to find her sleeping, looking like an angel. She bent down and kissed her warm, plump cheek and breathed in her smell, smiling at the sight of her precious daughter. She felt blessed.

For a few moments, Josie let herself think about Ivy's father, then quickly banished the thought. Some things were best left buried, she thought as she closed the door softly and asked Mildred if she would like to stay over.

Mildred looked tired and worried, but she didn't ask what Josie had found out in town. She readily accepted the invitation to spend the night on the couch. Josie wondered if Mildred stayed because she was concerned about her and Ivy. That would be like Mildred, Josie thought as she went to get the older woman a pillow and some bedding from the closet.

Too restless and wide awake to sleep, Josie went out on the porch and sat down on the step to stare up at the stars.

A pine-scented breeze skittered coolly across her bare arms, making goose bumps rise on her skin. She hugged herself. She'd done the right thing two years ago. The only thing she could do. No reason to start doubting herself now.

But she felt uneasy and knew it was more than just knowing Clay Jackson was in town or seeing some man in the trees the night before. It was the unshakable feeling that her past had come looking for her before she'd finished what she had to do. Before she could go home to Texas and face it as she'd planned.

She leaned back against the step and began counting the stars overhead, anything to distract her from thinking about Clay. Or worse, worrying about why he was in town.

Just an unhappy coincidence.

Right.

She caught the flicker of a light below her on the hillside not far from the stables and the creek.

Must be the owner of the ranch, Ruth Slocum, since she was the only other person here besides Mildred, and Mildred was snoring on the couch.

Josie sat up straighter. The faint light moved like a firefly through the dark. She watched it quickly disappear into the stables. Something must be wrong for Ruth to be in the stables this late at night. Odder yet, why had she come from the creek instead of her ranch house, which was in the opposite direction? Had one of the horses gotten out?

Worried, Josie got a flashlight from her truck and started down the hill.

The moon crested the mountains in a sky shot with stars. The breeze whispered through the tall, dew-damp grass, sending up the sweet scent of spring. Grass pulled at her boots, the night sky at her soul, making her feel small and insignificant.

She pushed open the stable door, surprised to find darkness. Reaching for the light switch, she stopped herself.

Through a crack in the tack room door at the end of the stables, she saw the flicker again of a flashlight, followed by a rustling sound.

She frowned and clicked on her own flashlight, keeping it aimed low at her feet as she moved slowly forward. Ruth wouldn't be rummaging around in the tack room at this time of the night. Not with a flashlight. Ruth had recently broken her ankle; even with her cane and walking cast, she had trouble getting around.

Just as those thoughts took hold—and their possible significance—Josie reached the tack room door. It hung open only a few inches, just enough that she could see a shadow moving around behind it and hear the thump of saddles being dropped to the floor.

But it was another sound that made her freeze.

This one behind her. The stable door she'd just come through opened with a rush of cool night air.

Startled, she swung around, banging the flashlight into a post with a resounding thud. The flashlight went out.

From inside the tack room, something fell or was dropped. The narrow beam of light blinked off, pitching the stables into a dense, silent dark.

She could feel the presence of the person who'd just entered the stables but couldn't see him. And she knew someone was still in the dark tack room, closer by. She held her breath, afraid to move.

Suddenly the tack room door flew open and a large, solid body hit her, sending her sprawling to the floor, knocking the air from her lungs. Whoever it was bolted for the nearby back door. A little of the yard light spilled in as a man-sized figure ran out, the door banging behind him.

Before she could get to her feet, someone tripped over her. She heard a loud male curse, then the sound of his body hitting the dirt. He quickly scrambled to his feet and ran toward the back door of the stables. The back door banged open again.

Before it could bang closed, the sound of a car engine roared to life, followed by another male curse. Then the sound of boot heels, slowly working their way back to her as the door banged shut again.

She was on all fours when the stable lights

flashed on. She looked up to see a large cowboy silhouetted against the bright light, his Stetson shadowing his face.

"What the hell?" the cowboy cursed.

She didn't need to see his face. She knew that body and that voice. Had heard that tone used in connection with her on numerous occasions.

Inwardly groaning, she hoisted herself to her feet, and dusting her backside, blinked as her eyes adjusted to the bright light. If anything, this close, he looked more handsome. Dark from his thick black hair to his eyes. His Spanish blood, although two generations removed, still fired passionately in his eyes. Unfortunately, that passion was almost always anger. "Hello, Jackson."

CLAY STARED IN STUNNED disbelief. He couldn't have been more shocked to see anyone. Hadn't he thought he'd seen her a couple hundred times over the past two years? Each time gave him a start. A jolt of pure electric shock that jump-started his heart and made it take off like an escaped con at the sound of a bloodhound.

"Josie." Even to his ears it sounded like a curse. He stared at her, assaulted with too many thoughts, too many memories and feelings.

Josie O'Malley. After all this time—and looking just as she had the last time he'd seen her. No, he realized as he studied her. She'd changed, although he couldn't put his finger on exactly how.

Her pale blond hair was still short and unruly, as if she'd just run her fingers through it. Her eyes were still that unbelievable blue. Clear as a Texas summer sky but unreadable as if the cool veneer masked a well of secrets. No doubt they did.

And she still had that defiant look, of course. She'd always been a spitfire. Rebellious, headstrong and willful as a wild mustang. Her father had actually thought Clay could do something with her. It had proved an impossible task. One he'd failed at miserably.

She was still slim and small, about five six in boots, but rounded. Actually more rounded than he remembered.

"What the hell are you doing here, Josie?" he demanded.

"What am *I* doing here?" she snapped, crossing her arms over the breasts he'd just been staring at. "What are *you* doing here is more to the point."

He jerked his gaze away, trying to make sense of this. But after one glance at the rear door of the stables, he narrowed his eyes at her again, seeing things a whole lot clearer. "*You* tripped me."

"Excuse me?" She hadn't lost her Texas twang—or her temper. Her blue eyes fired like forged steel. That was definitely something time hadn't changed.

Her first instinct was to tell him it wasn't any of his business. "I happen to work here."

"Work here?" he repeated, and glanced down the line of stalls.

She knew what he was thinking. That she shoveled manure—just as she had in his stables. What did she care what he thought? It made her more angry, though, that she *did* care.

"You work strange hours," he commented. "Or are you going to tell me that you just happened to be down here in the middle of the night, didn't bother to turn on the lights and just happened to be on the floor to trip me?"

She gritted her teeth, reminded of just how irritating this man could be. She bit off each word. "I saw a light and someone come in here so I walked down to check. I was just about to find out who when *you* came in and scared whoever it was away."

He raised an eyebrow.

"Whoever it was knocked me down and then you tripped over me," she continued, daring him to interrupt. "But that doesn't explain what *you're* doing here." What *was* he doing here? In Montana? But more important, on the ranch where she worked?

"I'm looking for someone."

She stared at him, her heart pounding. "Anyone in particular?"

"A thief," he said grudgingly. "I've been following him for the past four days. Unofficially, of course."

For a moment she'd thought he'd come to see her—even though she knew from watching him in town it wasn't true. When was she going to quit kidding herself when it came to this man?

"He led me from Texas to this stable."

She didn't like the sound of this. "Why would you follow a petty thief all the way from Texas?" She glanced toward the tack room. To this particular stable?

He frowned. "Petty? I don't think several million in jewels is petty, do you?"

Her heart looped in her chest. Hadn't she feared that the past had come looking for her? Worse yet, in the form of Clay Jackson, the one man she had reason to fear the most.

Did he just imagine the surprise that flashed in her eyes? The worry? God knows, he'd read more in her expression than he should have in the past.

She didn't answer. If anything, she seemed to be doing her best to look innocent. It was a look she'd perfected, but he knew her too well to fall for it.

"Actually, you know him," he said. Maybe had stayed in contact with him. "An old friend of *yours.*"

It was hard to tell if she really did pale under

the harsh light in the stable. Maybe he just wanted to see guilt in her eyes. Suspected it. Expected it. The same way he suspected she'd purposely tripped him to allow the thief to get away. After growing up next door to her, he'd have said he knew Josie O'Malley better than anyone.

But two years ago, she'd made him realize that he didn't know her as well as he'd thought.

"An old friend of *mine?*" she asked innocently.

Yes, he definitely glimpsed a crack in her composure. He smiled at her, but there was no humor behind it. Something hot tore at his insides. "You remember Raymond Degas," he said, studying her.

No doubt about it. The last of the color drained from her face.

"Raymond?"

"Come on, Josie," he prodded, his guts on fire. "You had to have heard about the jewel heist two years ago. Raymond and Odell were the number-one suspects. Raymond disappeared. Odell got himself killed. The jewels never turned up."

He felt frustration and anger burn in him. He'd held this woman at arm's length for years until two years ago. After Maria, he'd sworn he'd never let himself feel like that for a woman again.

But Josie had changed that. Damn her, she'd made him want her. Made him want *only* her. She'd dared him to love again, and just when he thought he might take the chance, she'd taken off. Without a word.

What made it worse was she'd disappeared right after the jewel heist.

It would have been suspicious enough if she hadn't been thick as thieves with Odell Burton and his buddy Raymond Degas at the time.

But Clay knew his suspicions ran much deeper. Deeper than he wanted to admit.

He watched her swallow, her gaze sliding away from his.

"I'm afraid I had other things on my mind two years ago," she said. She looked at him again, nothing showing in her face or her eyes now, as if she'd dropped a curtain over her emotions. He recalled the last time he'd seen her do that. Had she been trying to hide something then, too? The thought unnerved him.

But he had her now and he wasn't going to let go until he got the truth out of her. About everything.

Josie watched him glance toward the tack room.

"What do you suppose Raymond was doing in your tack?" he asked.

She didn't answer. She figured Clay had his own theories about that. She was shocked that Raymond had been here at all, let alone Clay.

"Suppose we take a look?" he said, indicating she could go first.

She thought about putting up an argument. Clay had no authority here. Nor did she take orders from him anymore—not that she ever had, without an argument. But she didn't want him forcing the issue by insisting they call the cops or wake up the ranch owner. The fewer people who knew about Clay Jackson and her past, the better. And she had a feeling that the thief hadn't found what he was looking for, anyway.

The tack room had been ransacked, all the tack and saddles pulled down in a heap in the middle of the floor.

"What would Raymond have wanted in here?" Clay said. "Have any ideas?"

Oh, she had lots of ideas, but none she wanted to share with him. She remembered the Lincoln Continental he'd been watching from the café in town. Was it Raymond's? But what would have brought Raymond to Three Forks? "Maybe he was looking for something to steal. You did say he was an alleged thief."

Clay smiled at her attempt at alleged humor. "Kind of a long drive to steal tack."

Had Clay really followed Raymond Degas all the way from Texas? All the way to the stables where she just happened to work? Quite a coincidence, if you believed in them. She had a feeling Clay didn't.

"Anything seem to be missing?" His tone made it clear he doubted it.

"We must have scared him away before he had a chance to steal something," she said, torn between despair and anger as he tried to provoke her.

"Convenient." He was eyeing her as if waiting for her to give him some answer.

Damn you, Jackson, she thought. *I don't owe you any explanations.* Well, at least not any she was willing to make. Including why she'd left Texas the way she had two years ago.

"Convenient that *you* just happened to scare him away when I reached the stables," he said, not willing to let it go. "And what a coincidence that Raymond Degas broke into the stable where you work."

She'd known that was coming.

"On top of that, you just happen to trip me and keep me from catching him," Clay finished, and crossed his arms, waiting, challenging her.

How much did this really have to do with the robbery? Clay hadn't wanted her, but he hadn't wanted anyone else to have her, either. She felt all that old resentment rising like steam off a geyser.

She thought of Ivy and blew out a long, heated breath. "You believe what you want. You always have."

She turned away and started out of the tack

room. She'd clean up the mess tomorrow. "If it was even Raymond," she added.

He moved in front of her, reminding her how fast he was on his feet as he blocked the door, blocked her exit. "It *was* Raymond." His voice was deep and soft and sent a chill through her as she was reminded of another time and place that Clay Jackson had been this close.

"Raymond led me all the way from Texas straight as a shot to you," Clay said, leaning closer, trapping her. "Come on, Josie. We both know what Raymond's looking for."

He was so close she could feel his breath against her cheek, smell his too-familiar male scent. Everything about him seemed to radiate a low-frequency electricity. She felt a buzz when she was around him and always had. But it seemed stronger somehow. More so than she remembered it.

"He's looking for the jewels."

She swallowed but said nothing, her nerves raw with the nearness of him. His body seemed to fill the tack room, making it as hot and sultry as a Texas summer night.

"That's right, you don't know anything about the robbery," he said, his tone clearly calling her a liar. "A rare collection of rubies, diamonds and emeralds, all irreplaceable. Intact, the jewelry would be impossible to fence. Too distinctive. Too easy to track. So what would the thieves do?"

How would she know? Why would she care? She knew nothing about getting rid of stolen property. And why did Clay Jackson *think* she did?

She shook her head, slowly, infinitesimally, afraid to move too much for fear of touching him. Or worse, him touching her.

He smiled. A halogen smile against the dark stubble of a day's growth of beard. He leaned so close it reminded her of the last time she'd seen him two years ago. He'd kissed her beside her barn in Texas. She didn't need the reminder. Not now. Not anymore.

She held her breath. But he didn't kiss her, although she did wonder if he, too, had been reminded of that kiss. Had purposely made her remember.

"It's hard to believe a petty small-time criminal like Raymond could pull off such a score, isn't it?" he said. "Even with the help of someone like Odell Burton."

She'd known Clay would get to Odell eventually. "I heard he was dead."

"Yeah, but he'd have needed an accomplice."

"Raymond."

He shook his head slowly, his smile gone. "I'm talking about someone smart. Someone who knew about the security plans and knew how to get them. Talk to me, Josie," he whispered. "Tell me what really happened that night."

Something in his voice, a slight break that could have been born of passion or pain, made her wonder which night he was referring to. She looked into his eyes and felt that old familiar rush. Like standing on the edge of a cliff. A combination of danger and exhilaration. Fear and longing. Her pulse pounded in her ears. Her heart drummed, the beat accelerating.

"Josie? Are you all right?"

They both turned at the sound of the voice behind them past the open tack room doorway. Mildred stood in the light, her expression worried. In her arms, she held a sleepy-eyed Ivy.

"Ivy woke and was frightened," Mildred said. "We came down to look for you—"

Clay stepped from the doorway and Josie rushed past him to take Ivy in her arms.

"Ma-ma," Ivy said, and snuggled against her.

Josie heard Clay's quick intake of breath as he came out of the tack room. She cradled her daughter to her, bracing herself as she turned and let her gaze rise to his.

He stared at her, then Ivy, his dark eyes wide with shock for the second time tonight. "I knew it," he whispered. "I damn well knew it."

"I understand you've already met my daughter Ivy," Josie said, bracing herself for the inevitable.

He dragged his gaze from Ivy's face to her own. His expression darkened, like a storm rolling in.

"I always wondered why you left Texas in such a hurry," he said, his words striking her like stones. "I guess I know now. At least one of the reasons. Did Odell know he had a daughter? Or is that just another of your well-kept secrets?"

Chapter Three

Josie with a baby! The same little girl he'd seen in town with the elderly baby-sitter he'd mistaken for a grandmother. Hadn't the toddler reminded him so much of Josie that he hadn't been able to resist taking a closer look?

But the little girl hadn't had Josie's incredible blue eyes. Now he realized that was because the baby had taken after her father. Odell.

He should have known. This at least explained part of Josie's hurried departure from Texas. No wonder she hadn't told her family.

He stared at Ivy for a long moment, surprised by the emotions that rushed him. She looked so much like her mother. In fact, she was the spitting image of Josie—except for the eyes.

This could have been my child.

The thought came out of left field, blindsiding him.

Josie hugged Ivy protectively to her, telling herself she shouldn't have been surprised. She should have known he'd see Odell in her daughter. Should have known he'd question if Odell had known she was pregnant. Still, she felt sick inside. What would he do now?

Or was that the least of her worries?

She looked into his angry face, trying hard to understand what it was about her that made him so angry with her. "Odell knew I was pregnant."

That seemed to surprise him. "You told him?"

"He guessed," she admitted.

Clay frowned. "That must have been what the two of you were arguing about that day by your barn. I'm sure Odell wanted nothing to do with a baby."

She looked down at her daughter. Ivy had fallen asleep again, her tiny cherub cheek warm and pink against Josie's shoulder, the dimpled arms locked around her neck. Odell had been furious about her pregnancy. She shivered at the memory of his threat.

When she looked up again, Clay's gaze seemed to soften. "So you struck out on your own. Just the two of you."

Was that grudging admiration she heard in his voice?

"What did you use for money, Josie? I know you didn't take much with you when you left."

So much for admiration. She knew what he was implying. "I *worked*."

"Pregnant?"

"I did what I had to do," she said stubbornly, unwilling to admit how she'd really managed alone, broke and pregnant. Unwilling because she was ashamed of what she'd done. And it really wasn't any of his business.

"You know I'm going to find out the truth."

"My life doesn't have anything to do with you." Even as she said it, she knew that wasn't true. Clay was definitely one of the reasons she'd left Texas.

"We should get the baby to bed," Mildred interrupted.

They both looked over at her. Clay seemed to have forgotten she was standing there, she'd been so quiet. And Josie had been distracted. Clay did that to her.

"Yes, you should get your baby to bed," Clay said. "But you and I aren't finished, Josie. Not by a long shot."

She feared that was true as she slipped past him and headed back up the hill to her cabin with Mildred beside her.

"Who is that man?" Mildred asked when they were out of earshot.

"A neighbor of my family's in Texas. I used to work for him."

Mildred said nothing, but Josie knew the older woman realized there was a lot more to it.

"He's the man I saw at the grocery store," Mildred said. "What does he want?" She sounded worried.

"He's here investigating a robbery."

"He's a policeman?" Mildred asked, sounding surprised but also relieved.

"No, he's a former deputy sheriff, but he's here unofficially." She could tell Mildred feared that he meant her or Ivy harm. "Don't worry. He'll catch his crook and be gone soon."

They walked in silence to the cabin, each lost in her own thoughts.

"You know, I might go on home, if you think you'll be all right tonight," Mildred said when they'd reached the cabin. "With all the excitement, I'm wide awake."

Josie understood perfectly. Mildred said she cleaned when she was upset. Something told Josie that Mildred's house was in for a scrubbin'. "We'll be fine."

Mildred bid her good-night after making certain that Josie had her pepper spray handy.

Josie watched her leave, worrying that Clay's departure wouldn't be that simple. Nothing with Clay had ever been simple. And she now had Raymond Degas to worry about as well.

As CLAY LEFT THE STABLES, he heard the high-pitched whinny of a horse. He looked toward the pasture and spotted a stallion standing in the moonlight watching him. The image gave him a start, the horse reminded him so much of Diablo. But while Diablo had been black as midnight, this horse was a blood bay. Like Diablo, though, it stood at least seventeen hands high and had that spirited, wild look in its eyes.

The stallion watched him warily, then took off as if touched with an electric prod, disappearing into the darkness, leaving Clay with one lasting impression. That horse was dangerous. Just like Diablo had been.

But he knew that wasn't why he'd gotten rid of Diablo. Even after the horse had almost killed him, he'd sold him because Diablo reminded him too much of Josie and an unforgettable dream he'd had about both of them.

Once at his truck, he drove up the road, parking out of sight of Josie's cabin. Then, taking his bed-roll, he cut through the pines until he could see the cabin without being seen. He tossed down the bag and plopped down on it.

Raymond Degas would be back. Not tonight, probably. But sometime. Clay was betting that Raymond hadn't found what he'd been looking for. And when he returned, Clay intended to be here.

When the lights blinked out in Josie's cabin, he

tried to get some sleep, but he couldn't quit think-ing about her.

Seeing her again had shaken him, much more than he wanted to admit. She was more beautiful than even he remembered. And the baby—

Odell's child, he reminded himself.

He tried to think about the jewels and his quest for them, rather than Josie. But it was impossible.

He'd often wondered if Josie had somehow been involved in the robbery. Raymond leading him right to her left little doubt that his suspicions about her had been warranted. It gave him no sat-isfaction, though.

But if she'd been in on the jewel heist, then why was Raymond rummaging around in the stables in the dark instead of just asking Josie for what he wanted?

Clay swore. Unless Josie had double-crossed Odell and Raymond and taken the jewels.

That seemed pretty far-fetched, considering the woman was pregnant at the time. But with Josie O'Malley he wouldn't rule out anything.

He even blamed her for the dream that had plagued him for the past two years. A dream he now thought of as That Damned Dream.

He'd started having the dream after being bucked off Diablo not once—but twice in twenty-four hours. The dream was always the same: Josie O'Malley riding through a creek toward him on the large black horse, the Texas hill country behind her, the horse's hooves throwing up water droplets that hung in the moonlight. Josie coming out of the darkness of the live oaks and into the moonlight, wearing a yellow dress, her shoulders bare, the wet cotton clinging to her skin. She was buck-naked beneath the dress! Her nipples dark and hard, pressing against the soaked fabric as she dismounted and came to him where he'd fallen from the horse, her blue eyes filled with a longing that matched his own.

Definitely a fantasy dream. It disturbed him that he'd had it at all. He'd never thought of Josie like…that. Nor did he want to.

On top of that, the dream mocked him with the incredible impossibility of it. Josie had been riding the horse that had thrown him and then run off—Diablo, his wild green-broke stallion, and she was way too inexperienced to ride a horse like that, let alone one as unpredictable as Diablo.

He'd awoken the next morning, horseless, with a knot the size of Texas on his head, a terrible headache and no memory of what had happened. But with the ground under him instead of a horse, he had a pretty good idea what had taken place.

It had been a fool thing, trying to ride Diablo. Especially in the mood he'd been in. He'd caught Odell Burton in his barn with Josie, gotten into a fight with him and made Josie mad. Although he'd won the fight, he still had the scar where Odell's ring had cut him.

In a foul mood by that time, he'd gotten half drunk and decided to ride Diablo. Not his best decision.

The next morning when he limped back to the ranch, he'd seen Josie—again with Odell, but he'd had the good sense to stay clear of them both.

That's when he started having That Damned Dream. The last thing he'd needed was Josie O'Malley in his dreams. Having her around his ranch was trouble enough without conjuring up the feel, smell and taste of her the moment he closed his eyes.

On top of that, she didn't get over being mad at him from what he could tell. He and Josie had argued enough over how to break horses.

Six weeks later, the jewels were stolen from the Williams Gallery in town where the collection was to go on display. He'd acted as a consultant on the security plans. In fact, he had a copy of the plans in his locked desk drawer at the ranch.

That's when the first inkling of suspicion about Josie started. When Brandon Williams, the jewel collector, called to ask if Clay still had his copy. Williams felt the only way the thieves could have pulled off the heist was with the plans.

When Clay had gone to his desk, he'd found the plans—but someone had been in the locked drawer. They'd used a key, because the lock hadn't been tampered with—and he had the only key.

He'd assured Brandon Williams that his plans were there, keeping his suspicions to himself. Temporarily.

With Odell Burton and Raymond Degas wanted for questioning in the heist, Clay wondered if one of them could have somehow gotten his keys. That seemed impossible. But Odell was always hanging around Josie.

He'd saddled up and ridden over to the O'Malley ranch. Josie was by the barn. Clay wasn't surprised when Odell came out of the barn, looking angry.

He rode toward them, unable to hear their words, but he could see that they were obviously arguing. Odell had grabbed Josie's arm, and she seemed to be trying to fight him off.

Odell spotted him as he rode up and took off before Clay's boot soles hit the dust beside Josie.

"Don't" was all Josie said when she saw him. She was crying and upset.

Without thinking, he'd pulled her into his arms and kissed her. A crazy impulse. He hadn't known it at the time, but it would be the last time he'd see her until today. It had been one amazing good-bye kiss.

After it was over, she'd pulled back, confusion

in her gaze. Her eyes had filled with tears. "What do you want from me, Jackson?"

When he didn't answer, she spun on her heel and left him standing with his reins in his hand.

He'd watched her go, fighting the urge to go after her. What *did* he want from her? He'd told himself he didn't know. Getting involved with Josie O'Malley was definitely out of the question. So he'd swung up into the saddle and ridden off, kicking himself for kissing her.

The next day he'd discovered that she'd packed up and left Texas, lock, stock and barrel. At the time, he'd blamed himself. For kissing her. For being jealous and possessive when he had no right. For being angry with her for making him want her. Because by then, he'd realized that he did want her. Like he'd never wanted any woman before. He just wasn't fool enough to confuse that with love and all that went with it.

A week later Odell was killed in a fiery car crash. Raymond Degas had already disappeared, just like Josie. And the jewels had never been found.

He'd been suspicious of Josie's timing when she'd left. But now as he stared down at the cabin below him on the hillside, he didn't kid himself that she wasn't somehow involved, and damned if he'd let any feelings for her or her baby keep him from proving it.

In the wee hours of the morning, he finally dropped off into a bottomless sleep. In the dream, Josie rode to him on a dark stallion, coming out of the creek, her dress wet and clinging to her naked body. A body he knew as well as his own.

Clay woke, heart pounding, drenched with sweat. The bright sun told him it was morning. His aching head and the lingering memory of the dream assured him it wasn't going to be a good day.

Chapter Four

He bathed in the icy creek, hoping the cold would rid him of the images of Josie, her body flushed with desire. But while the freezing-cold water curbed his desire temporarily, it did nothing for his mood.

He called Texas, dialing Brandon Williams's number. Four days ago when he'd called Williams to tell him that he'd gotten a lead on the stolen jewels, the man hadn't been exactly appreciative.

"I'd put that unfortunate incident behind me," he snapped. "Nice of you to call and remind me of my loss."

Williams, a physically fit man in his late forties with a small fortune and an appetite for expensive things, was a pain in the neck. Clay couldn't wait until he could return the jewels to the obnoxious man and hopefully prove to himself that the thieves hadn't gotten the security plans from his desk.

"I got a lead on Raymond Degas."

That had definitely surprised Williams. "Really? Where is he?"

"On the move. I intend to stay with him and see where he takes me."

Williams believed he'd never see his precious jewels again. That was enough of a challenge for Clay, even if he hadn't felt he might be responsible.

"Have you found my jewels?" Williams asked now without preamble.

He gritted his teeth, his already-bad mood darkening. He wished now he hadn't promised to call Williams daily. He wanted to say, "Get the money ready to return to the insurance company," but instead he said, "Not yet." With Raymond out of hiding, Clay had the feeling that it was just a matter of time before he found the jewels, and he couldn't wait to see Williams's face when he handed them to him.

"I'm making progress," he told Williams. "He broke into a local ranch here last night."

"Really?" Williams actually sounded interested.

Clay told him about the tack room break-in, but left out anything about Josie. He didn't want Williams to know that he suspected Josie, let alone that Raymond led him right to her.

"Keep me informed," Williams ordered, and hung up.

Clay turned off his cell phone and cursed. He wanted this over with as quickly as possible. Also, the less time he spent around Josie, the better. He knew Josie felt the same way about him.

He finished dressing and rubbed his jaw. He needed a shave and a decent night's sleep. As he headed toward her cabin, his stomach growled and he added food to his list of needs. He could smell coffee and cinnamon toast. He stopped at the sight of Josie on the porch, having breakfast with Ivy. A shave, food and sleep weren't all he needed.

His conviction to nail her for the robbery faltered as he watched her with her daughter, watched how loving, tender, patient and sweet she was with Ivy.

He smiled at one distinct memory of her as a kid trying to ride some rough stock her father and older brothers had forbidden her to go near. He'd watched her from the fence rail, knowing the minute her father and brothers turned their backs, she'd try to ride that blamed green horse.

She hated anyone to tell her she couldn't do something and she resented her bossy brothers. Unfortunately, that day she'd gotten bucked off and broken her arm. But Clay had always admired her grit.

He frowned and pushed the memory away, reminding himself that she was now in a different trouble league. Jewel theft. And this time, he wasn't silently cheering her on from the sidelines. He was the one who'd have to take her down, and he feared she was up to her pretty little neck in this mess. He just hadn't figured how yet.

When the blue Honda drove up and the woman he'd seen last night in the stables went up to the cabin to stay with Ivy, he followed Josie down to the stables, keeping himself hidden. He figured she knew he'd be around and fairly close, but he didn't want her to see him. Not yet, anyway.

He'd expected her to disappear into the stables for several hours of horse feeding and stable cleaning. Instead she reappeared moments later, leading the wild stallion he'd seen last night toward a round, enclosed pen. The horse jerked at the halter she had on him and snorted and kicked.

His chest constricted. Anyone could see that the stallion was dangerous. Especially in the wrong hands. What did Josie think she was going to do with the beast?

He followed her until she disappeared into the door of the pen, the stallion obviously upset and anxious. On the far side of the building, he found another door. Inside, a small viewing area had been cut out of the side of the enclosure. He opened the door and slipped in. The area was small with a single bench. It ran in front of a long, narrow window that looked down into the pen. He didn't sit but stayed back in the shadows to watch.

Josie stopped in the center of the circular pen to rub the flat of her hand over the horse's forehead, her movements slow, graceful, gentle. The stallion snorted and jerked his head, ears up and back as Josie slid off the halter.

Sensing its freedom, the stallion took off, running around in a circle, obviously nervous and tense.

Josie pulled a coil of light rope from beneath her jeans jacket and let the bulk of it drop to the dirt floor. The horse eyed her, looking as wary as Clay felt. Josie held the stallion's gaze as, from the center of the pen, she began to pitch the line at the horse's flank, sending him cantering around her.

What the hell did she think she was doing? A horse like that could be unpredictable. Dangerous. At any moment, the stallion could turn on her and kill her before she could get out.

"Fool woman," he cursed.

He spun around at the sound of a soft chuckle behind him to find an elderly woman with a cane standing in the doorway. She didn't seem surprised to see him as she let the door close behind her.

"Are you familiar with this type of horse training?" she asked, her voice stronger than he'd expected. She was tall, rawboned and weathered, with sharp eyes and a determined air about her. A horsewoman. She used the cane to maneuver herself over to the window and the bench in front of it. She wore a walking cast on her left ankle and seemed to belong here. He took her for the ranch owner.

"I've heard about it," he said.

She chuckled again as she took a seat on the bench. "Please join me."

He wondered if she had any idea who he was. Or what he was doing here. She didn't seem to care as he sat next to her. Her attention was on what was happening in the ring below them.

Anxiously, he watched Josie pitch the line at the stallion as he cantered around the fifty-foot circle. The horse watched Josie as closely as she appeared to be watching him.

Suddenly she flicked the line in front of him. The stallion swung around and ran in the opposite direction, keeping close to the wall, his eye still on her.

"Watch his inside ear," the elderly woman said as she leaned forward on her cane.

To his surprise, while the stallion's outside ear continued to monitor his surroundings, the inside ear locked on Josie.

"Watch his head," the woman ordered.

The stallion dipped his head, turning it slightly toward Josie, and settled into a steady trot.

"He'll start licking and chewing and running his tongue outside his mouth," the older woman predicted.

Sure enough.

"It's a show of respect," the woman said, looking over at him. "And a willingness to cooperate."

Clay sat up, leaning toward the window as Josie dropped the line, then angled both her body and her gaze away from the horse. The stallion slowed, then stopped to look at her.

Clay held his breath. Josie seemed so small inside the pen with the powerful horse. Too small.

Then she did something Clay couldn't believe. She turned her back on the stallion.

"Fool woman," he breathed, his heart pounding as he feared what the horse would do. "She's going to get herself killed."

"Then you don't know Josie O'Malley," the woman said as she put a hand on his arm to keep him from rising.

The stallion approached Josie from behind, but she didn't turn. Just inches away, the horse reached out with his large head. Clay held his breath, his heart pounding.

The stallion touched his nose to Josie's shoulder. She turned slowly, and he watched as the horse let her rub the spot between his eyes.

Amazing. Josie had this high-strung, unbroken horse eating out of her hand. He stared in disbelief as she turned and walked away and the stallion followed her like a pet dog.

He wouldn't have believed it, especially after

seeing the stallion in the corral last night. The horse had had that wild look—the same look Clay had glimpsed in Josie's eyes a time or two.

But now as he watched her, a thought hit him right between the eyes like a brick. The way she handled that stallion… If Josie had been able to tame that wild stallion, then maybe she'd somehow been able to smooth-talk Diablo into letting her ride him.

"Well?" the elderly woman asked, jerking him back from the thought.

"She must have worked with the horse before," Clay said, unwilling to accept what he'd just seen.

"Are you always so skeptical and suspicious?" the woman beside him asked, those keen eyes on him.

"I just know that horses are like women. Unpredictable. Often dangerous. And it's usually a mistake to turn your back on them."

She laughed and held out her hand. "Ruth Slocum. Owner of the Buffalo Jump Ranch. And you are…"

"Clay Jackson," he said, not at all surprised by the strength he found in her handshake.

She slanted her head, still openly studying him. "I understand you're here investigating a crime?"

"Unofficially. I followed a suspected jewel thief to your stables last night." He didn't mention his suspicions about Josie. Not yet.

"I heard someone got into the tack room, but a jewel thief? What would a jewel thief want in my stables?"

"That's the question, isn't it?" he said, glancing down into the pen at Josie.

Ruth Slocum followed his gaze but said nothing.

Chapter Five

"He's certainly a handsome devil," Ruth said as she sat down to the table on Josie's porch.

"Don't say that too loudly," Josie warned as she slid Ivy into her high chair. "It's a bad idea to feed *that* man's ego, and knowing him, he isn't far away."

Her boss smiled. "What about feeding his stomach? I heard it growling while we were watching you gentle that new stallion this morning."

Josie looked up in surprise, almost dropping the bowl of macaroni salad she'd whipped up for their lunch. "Jackson watched?"

"You seem surprised," Ruth said.

She'd known he'd hang around, but she never dreamed he'd have any interest in her work. "He and I never agreed on horse training. Or much of anything else for that matter." She handed the bowl to Mildred, who was already seated but hadn't said much.

"I think he's here to make trouble for Josie and Ivy," Mildred blurted.

Ruth raised a brow at her friend. "Oh, you do, do you?" She chuckled. "What do you think, Josie?"

She felt the woman's sharp eyes on her as she sat down. "I think he's on a wild-goose chase. But I hope he finds what he's looking for soon and leaves."

Ruth nodded and glanced toward the pines behind the cabin. "Don't you think you should invite him to lunch?"

"With us?" Mildred asked, apparently shocked that her old friend would want to share the table with him.

"Better to have him where we can see him, don't you think?" Ruth said.

Josie hesitated. She could tell that Ruth was taken with Clay, although other than his looks, she couldn't image why. But not asking him to lunch would look as if she had reason to avoid the man. Which was true. Or that she had something to hide. Ditto.

She pushed back her chair and went to the edge of the porch. "Jackson!" she hollered. "You might as well come join us for lunch."

Silence.

"Try, please," Ruth whispered.

She mugged a face at her boss but obliged. "Please?"

He came down out of the pines and at least had the good grace to look sheepish.

She couldn't help laughing as she shook her head at him and went to get another place setting.

"Thank you for the kind invitation," he said, tipping his hat to the ladies at the table and giving Josie his best smile when she returned with a plate and silverware. Ivy giggled and turned shy as he pulled up an extra chair and sat down next to her high chair on the opposite side of Josie.

They talked about the weather, horses and kids during the meal. Mostly Clay charmed Ruth, even softened up Mildred, and did his best to put Josie at ease.

But unlike the other women, Josie knew the threat he posed. She secretly hoped that Clay was wrong. That the man in the stables last night hadn't been Raymond Degas. And that no matter who it had been, it had nothing to do with the stolen jewels. Or Texas.

But, like him, she couldn't pretend it wasn't an amazing coincidence that Raymond—or at least the man Clay believed was Raymond Degas—had led Clay to her.

The one woman at the table whom Clay charmed without any effort was Ivy. She definitely had taken to him, just as Mildred had said after their encounter in the grocery store.

And Clay, to her amazement, seemed to have a real way with the toddler. Who would have known? Josie had never seen him show any interest in children before. Or was it just Ivy?

The thought worried her. She told herself that her daughter just had that kind of effect on people. She was as much a charmer as Clay. It surprised her, though, that Clay Jackson would be susceptible to that charm. Maybe he did have a heart after all. Scary thought.

After they'd finished, Ruth offered to clear the table with Mildred's help. When they'd both disappeared inside the cabin, he asked, "Where'd you learn to break horses like that?"

She looked up from removing Ivy's bib and felt the heat of his gaze. "I don't actually *break* them. I try to gentle them, to gain their trust and confidence so they let me train them."

He smiled. "I'm familiar with the approach. I suppose it works sometimes, if you get lucky."

She felt a surge of anger. "You just can't admit that I might know what I'm doing when it comes to horses, can you?"

He met her gaze and held it, his smile fading, his eyes growing dark and serious. "You were great with that horse this morning," he said, as if the words came hard. "Where did you learn that?"

She busied herself with Ivy again. "I've always loved horses, you know that. I used to watch my father and brothers."

She knew he wasn't buying it. "The O'Malley men don't *gentle* horses."

How true. "I also learned a lot watching your trainers, and I've read about the different techniques. The rest Ruth taught me."

"Really," he said, surprise in his voice. "So you learned some of it in Texas?"

She nodded, wanting to change the subject. "I really need to get back to work."

He got up from the table, studying her openly.

She knew he was wondering if she'd ever worked with his horses. He no doubt couldn't stand the thought that she'd ridden one of them.

She carried Ivy into the cabin. Clay jumped up to open the door and followed her inside, obviously not done with his interrogation.

"Ruth said you'd never worked with that horse before today," he said.

"You don't think *Ruth* would lie to you, do you?"

"It's not that I doubted you—"

Right. She played patty-cake with Ivy, changed her and got her ready for her nap, although Mildred insisted she'd be happy to do it. Josie wanted the time with Ivy. She kissed her daughter and laid her down in the crib.

"Singa," Ivy cried.

Josie glanced at Clay, who had followed her into Ivy's room. She felt self-conscious, but she wasn't going to let him disrupt the life she'd made for them any more than she could help.

She sang Ivy's favorite song, one Josie's father used to sing to her when she was a child. Suddenly she felt close to tears, her homesickness for Texas, the ranch, but especially her father and brothers, acute.

"You have a beautiful voice," Clay said as she turned away to hide her tears and tuck her daughter in.

When she turned back, he was gone, the screen door downstairs banging behind him. Ruth came in to give Ivy a kiss and took Josie's arm as they walked out of the room.

Ruth Slocum had given her more than a job. She'd recognized her love of horses and her desperate need to do something with her life for her unborn baby.

Ruth had advertised for a stable hand, and Josie had driven out to the ranch with little hope that anyone was going to hire her in her obviously pregnant state.

While Ruth showed her around the stables, Josie hadn't been able to keep her hands off of the horses. It had been weeks by then since she'd been around horses. She'd missed the smell, the sound, the sight, but especially the feel of them. Under her palms. Under her saddle.

Later Ruth would tell her that it was her love for horses that made her offer Josie the job, which included a place to live on the ranch. Within days, Ruth pulled her out of the stables and into the training pen.

In the pen, Ruth had taught Josie more about horses than she dreamed possible and made her realize how much more she needed to learn. Horse training took a lifetime, Ruth had told her, but Josie knew now that it was what she wanted to do with her life, along with raising Ivy. Horses and her daughter *were* her life. She had no regrets about that. Only a deep sense of gratitude to Ruth.

She'd met Mildred through Ruth. The two older women had been friends since grade school. Both had been godsends to Josie. Along with giving her a job and a place to live, Ruth had dug out her son's crib from the attic, and Mildred had collected clothing from her many nieces' and nephews' children for Ivy.

Josie often wondered how she'd have ever made it without both women. She just hoped that one day she'd be able to repay their kindnesses.

"Mind if I offer a little advice?" Ruth asked now.

Josie shook her head.

"Men are like horses," she said. "What works with horses, also works with men."

Josie blinked at her. "You aren't suggesting that I try to…gentle Clay Jackson to a saddle?"

The older woman laughed. "Hell, yes. If you can communicate with a horse by reading his body language and sending similar signals back, why not do the same with a man?"

"I don't have to read Clay's body language, I can read his lips loud and clear," she said, feeling tears close to the surface. "He always thinks the worst of me."

Ruth tilted her head to study her. "What kind of signals are you sending *him?*"

"You don't understand. There was a man in my past—"

Ruth laughed, her weathered face crinkling with humor. "Honey, it's pretty obvious there was at least one man in your past."

Josie had to smile in spite of herself. "There's a lot you don't know about Clay and me."

"And there's a lot I do," Ruth said, squeezing her hand. "Would you give up on a horse after a few failed attempts? You have to school a horse, slowly and gently. Men are no different, honey."

Josie smiled at the idea of schooling Clay Jackson.

"You have a gift when it comes to horses, Josie."

"Yeah, well, believe me, I don't have the same gift when it comes to men."

Ruth laughed and released her hand. "Give it a chance. I think you'll be surprised."

As Ruth left, Mildred settled into the couch with her knitting. She made afghans for her church as part of a blankets-for-the-homeless project and swore that knitting kept her out of trouble. Josie thought she might take it up.

As she pushed open the screen door, she wasn't surprised to find Clay leaning against one of the posts, looking toward the stables. In the distance, Ruth drove off in the golf cart she used to get around the ranch.

"Thanks for lunch. It was delicious," Clay said, never forgetting his breeding or his southern manners. Old-school Texans and cowboys prided themselves on their manners.

"It was Ruth's idea."

"I'll have to thank Ruth the next time I see her."

She groaned, hoping he wouldn't be around long enough. "Don't you have something better to do than follow me around, Jackson?" she snapped irritably as he fell in beside her for the walk down to the stables.

"Nope. You *are* my work, Josie. And believe me, it isn't easy. As a matter of fact, I've been thinking—"

"I'll just bet you have," she said, giving him a sweet-as-penuche smile.

"You really should smile more often," he said. "You're really quite attractive when you're not frowning."

She glared over at him.

"Sorry, just trying to help," he said with a shrug.

"I'll have you know that I've been doing fine on my own. I don't need your help. Or your advice." She started to walk away from him.

He grabbed her arm and pulled her around to face him. "What makes you so damned ornery?"

"I've been bossed around my whole life," she snapped, jerking her arm free. "By my father. By my three older brothers." Her gaze narrowed. "And by you. Everyone knows what's best for me. Even you treated me like I was one of your horses that needed to be corralled."

"I treat my horses very well."

"Oh!" she said, stomping away from him.

He shook his head as he stared at her rigid spine, the proud incline of her head. A woman with a lot of grit. Then he laughed softly and went after her. "A man can't act protective around you."

"It's more than that, Jackson, and you know it."

Damn her. She knew him too well. Although there was a lot she didn't understand about him.

But she was right about one thing. He wasn't

here to protect her. Nor did he have any business trying to tame her in Texas. "I was out of line."

That took some of the wind out of her sails. She'd obviously expected him to make excuses. She slowed, studying him as if she suspected he wasn't being entirely honest.

He couldn't remember a time he'd been more honest.

"I didn't want to see you hurt. Odell Burton was nothing but trouble and you were—"

"Wild as an unbroke stallion? Isn't that what you once told me?"

He wished he could take back some of the things he'd said to her. "Wilder," he admitted. "But I was going to say young, just a kid."

She stopped abruptly and turned, hands on her hips. "Well, I'm not a kid anymore."

"You can say that again!" He let out a low whistle.

She narrowed her gaze at him. "What is it about me that scares you so much?"

He laughed. "Everything about you scares me, Josie."

She shook her head at him, thinking he was joking, and turned and headed on down the hill to the stables.

He caught up with her in two easy strides. "You have to understand, Josie. I care about you. But I'm going to find those jewels and who helped

Odell and Raymond steal them. I have the feeling that I'm getting close. I think I'm making some people nervous.''

She wagged her head at him, not looking the least bit nervous. ''You're so sure of yourself, aren't you, Jackson. But if Odell and Raymond *did* pull off the robbery, why couldn't they have gotten rid of the jewels a long time ago? What would be the purpose in waiting so long? They don't strike me as men with a lot of patience. And if they are the fools you think they are, why didn't they try to fence the jewels?''

He'd already wondered the same thing. ''You make a very good argument.'' And she'd known both men better than he had. All he had was his gut instinct. His gut instinct and Raymond Degas had gotten him this far. Straight to Josie O'Malley. ''I *will* find the jewels.''

''That's all that matters, isn't it?''

He met her gaze. ''Yes. I need to know who stole them and how they did it. I have a theory that the thieves got to the security plans in my office at the ranch.''

Nothing showed in her expression, but her eyes seemed a shade darker blue.

''I'm not going back to Texas until I get both. And you're going to help me.''

She shot him a disbelieving look. ''Why would I do *that?*''

He arched a brow at her. "To prove that you had nothing to do with the robbery. If you have nothing to hide—"

Her gaze narrowed, hotter than a summer afternoon. "I forgot, I'm always guilty until proven innocent with you."

"Raymond didn't get what he came here for," Clay said, angry with her for trying to make *him* feel guilty. "He'll be back. I intend to be here. One way or the other."

"I see," she said, biting off each word. "What is it you want from me?"

What he'd dreamed he'd had one night on a creek bank in Texas. But that was pure fantasy, and most of the time, he knew it. "Just the truth, Josie."

Anger flashed in her gaze. "You sure you can handle the truth, Jackson?"

She had him there. "I also thought you might want me to stay in the cabin so I'd be close by if you needed me."

She laughed. "Well, then you thought wrong," she said, turning her back on him as she stalked away, her hips swaying in her tight-fitting jeans.

Could he handle the truth? He damn sure hoped so.

THE AFTERNOON PASSED slowly, with Clay watching her every move. She finally quit early and went up to the cabin to prepare supper. Clay didn't make any effort to pretend he wasn't watching her like a hawk or that he wasn't still hoping to be invited inside.

Fat chance.

She walked away from him a few yards from the cabin, and when she looked back, he was gone. But not far, she knew.

She made his favorite meal, opening the kitchen window to let the smell waft out to him. Let him eat his heart out. Let him go hungry. Let him suffer.

She'd planned to spend the evening with Ivy, but Mildred reminded her that the two of them were expected over at the neighbor's for a birthday party.

Ivy and the little neighbor girl, Rachel, were the same age, and Mildred often got them together to play. "She gets sick of all us adults around," Mildred would say of Ivy.

Josie didn't want Ivy to go, and Mildred must have noticed.

"We won't be late. It's good for Ivy to be around other kids," Mildred said.

She couldn't argue that. She just felt uneasy. As if a storm were blowing in. But the sky was clear. Not a cloud in the dwindling blue. The only storm that had blown in was Clay Jackson.

After Mildred and Ivy left, the cabin seemed too

quiet, especially knowing that Clay was out there. She tried to read, but was too restless to concentrate.

She knew there was only one thing that would relax her. Even though it was getting dark, she headed for the stables.

HE LIKED THE DARK. The vast emptiness of night. It had a familiar universal appeal. It defied reality. He could pretend he was in Texas. He could pretend he was deep underground.

He felt a small thrill at the thought. But as much as he liked the dark, it didn't do for him what the caves did. He couldn't wait to get back into the caverns. Except next time, he wasn't going alone. Next time he'd have Ivy O'Malley with him.

He smiled at the thought, because it wasn't the toddler he was thinking about but her mother. Ivy was only a means to an end. He'd known for a long time what he wanted. What he deserved. Now he knew how to get it.

He waited until the last of the sun died away before he moved. He preferred moving under the cloak of darkness. Like a vampire coming out of his casket, he felt ready to roam with the disappearing light. He felt an infinity with the night as if it brought him to life and made him invisible. Maybe even invincible.

He definitely felt stronger, more powerful.

Ready. Ready to give Josie O'Malley just what she had coming to her. The thought made him salivate. He felt the familiar tightening in his loins, the hammering in his chest. Expectation. He couldn't wait to see her face. She'd taken so much from him.

Eventually he'd take what she cherished most. Take Ivy to a place of endless darkness. And Josie would follow. Josie.

And Clay Jackson.

He swore softly under his breath. Hadn't he always known he'd have to do something about Jackson?

He breathed in the night, shifting his thoughts to something more pleasant. It was hard not to rush his plans. Not to make mistakes.

But part of the fun was the anticipation, the planning. Unfortunately, he had a couple of flies in the ointment he'd have to deal with first. He wouldn't let anyone mess this up. Not again. He was too close.

As he moved through the darkness, the moon shimmered off the rock bluffs behind the ranch. He considered how he would kill Clay Jackson. He just wished he'd done it a long time ago.

Chapter Six

Josie felt a prickling along her neck as she neared the stables. A feeling that she wasn't alone and that someone other than Clay was out there.

She glanced around the ranch yard. Horses shifted restlessly in the corral. A cloud moved across the moon, extinguishing any light. Closer, a breeze ruffled her short hair and sent a chill down her back.

Cautiously she pushed open the door, gripping the flashlight she carried, realizing it made a lousy weapon. Raymond must have come back, just as Clay had predicted.

A sound came from out of the darkness.

"Who's there?" she called out.

Silence. Then she heard the scrape of boots as someone approached, but in the opposite direction from where she'd thought she'd heard something.

A cowboy rounded the corner, his western hat slanted low over his face. As he shoved the hat back, she half expected to see Raymond Degas's face.

"I figured you'd want to go for a ride," Clay drawled. "I was hoping for an invitation."

Her first instinct was to be rude. But she was too relieved it'd only been Clay. Also, as jumpy as she was, she didn't really mind if he rode with her tonight.

She just needed to get out, to feel the freedom of being on a horse. And she figured she couldn't get rid of him no matter what she did. She might as well have him where she could see him, as Ruth had suggested.

"I guess you might as well," she said, heading for the tack room. "You're determined to hang around, anyway."

He laughed as he joined her in the tack room, filling up the small space with his presence. "With an invitation like that, how can I refuse?"

She shoved a saddle at him, feeling his gaze on her. She didn't dare lift her eyes to his. "You can ride Lady. She's about your speed."

He backed out of the tack room. "You're too kind."

"I'd hate to see you on your backside." Again. She remembered the last time she'd watched him try to ride Diablo at his ranch in Texas.

"I'd think you'd have had your fill of horses for the day," he said as they saddled up.

"I could never get my fill of horses. They're intelligent, graceful and loyal, with a willing nature." Everything that men weren't.

And she'd always loved to ride at night. Now she usually rode in the afternoons, taking Ivy with her. But she missed riding hard and fast under a vast night sky. She used to believe she could outrun her troubles. She didn't anymore.

THE NIGHT WAS DARK, only the faint hint of the moon hidden behind a thick bank of clouds as they rode out. No stars. Just shades of darkness splattered across the tall grass.

Clay rode out ahead of her. She'd always loved seeing him in the saddle. He rode tall, assured, as at home on a horse as he was anywhere. Sometimes he seemed to love horses as much as she did. Those times she felt herself soften toward him. A pull stronger than gravity.

She'd felt the same way earlier, watching him with Ivy. Who knew the man could possess such tenderness?

She let the wind blow back her hair as she loped across the field to catch him. The breeze caressed her face, the horse beneath her soothed her, and the night seemed filled with an electric excitement.

He seemed as lost as she was in the ride, his face turned to the black rough line of the mountain peaks and the clouds that hung like a shroud over them, hiding more than the moon from the night, making the vast landscape seem smaller, almost intimate.

They didn't speak as they rode toward the light-colored bluffs of the old buffalo jump. The darkness felt thick with an eager silence as if holding its breath.

Josie brought her horse to a halt at the bottom of the cliffs and climbed down to stare up at the rough rock face. She often rode up here, thinking sometimes she could feel the history that lingered like the dying sun on the rocks. Tonight, though, she felt nothing but the man beside her as Clay dismounted and joined her.

She sensed his body heat as if it were drawing toward her. The masculine scent of him mixed with the smell of leather and horses. Intoxicating. Her body felt alive, everything magnified as if this were her first night here, as if she were experiencing it all for the first time. Seeing it, feeling it, sensing it not only through her own eyes but through his as well.

He was close. Too close. To her. To the truth.

''Thank you for bringing me here,'' he said, his voice sounding hoarse with unexpected emotion. He knew that this place was special to her, the same way he'd known she'd want to ride tonight. He knew her, better than any man ever had. And yet, he didn't know her at all.

She looked over at him, surprised that he understood what this place meant to her.

He smiled, acknowledging that surprise. But it was a sad smile full of regret.

She wanted to say something, but the moment seemed lost. Was Ruth right? Had she misjudged him? Just as he had her? Was that why it surprised her when he knew anything halfway good about her?

"We'd better get back," she said, mounting up. She hated to cut her ride short, but she realized this had been a bad idea. Being alone with Clay only reminded her of Texas and the past.

She rode toward the Madison River and the ranch, letting the horse run, thankful Clay didn't try to catch up to her or, worse yet, try to talk to her. She didn't like the feeling that she might be wrong about him. Wrong about herself.

She reminded herself why Clay was here. To find the jewels. And the thieves. If she was smart, she'd be very careful. Thinking of Clay as anything other than the enemy would be a huge mistake. One she'd made once before. And look how that had turned out.

She raced through the tall grass, letting the horse go, the wind roaring past along with the darkness. In the distance she could see the ranch, the yard light glowing.

She headed for it, knowing Clay wasn't far behind, and slowed to let her horse cool down.

But Clay didn't catch her until she reached the ranch yard. She pulled up short when she saw the expression on his face.

"What is it?" she asked in a whisper, his gaze scaring her.

He stared at her as if seeing a stranger. Did he really know this woman? It appeared not. But at the same time, he wondered if he knew her even better than he thought he did. Much better.

"Nothing's wrong," he said, unable to take his eyes off her. "Why?"

She eyed him for a moment, then shook her head and dismounted to lead her horse toward the stables.

"You ride very well," he commented, trying to hide the true extent of his surprise as he dismounted and followed her toward the stables.

He'd never known she could ride like that. He'd watched her gallop across the pasture, the dim moonlight illuminating only her pale blond hair and the light-colored flanks of the horse beneath her. She looked like a spirit, some night sprite. Just the reflection of a woman on a horse riding through the night.

Stunned, he realized he'd seen her ride like this once before. His heart quickened, his pulse pounding at his temple as he remembered Josie in the dream. And then in the pen earlier with the unbroken stallion.

It *was* possible that Josie had ridden Diablo.

The realization hit him hard, filling his head with all the implications. *If* she could gentle a stallion like she had today, *if* she could ride like she had tonight, *if* she *had* ridden Diablo that night in Texas—

"Are you all right?"

Her voice dragged him from his thoughts. He looked down at her. She stood next to him, looking at him with concern in her gaze.

"I'm fine," he lied as he reminded himself of all the reasons that night had been nothing more than a dream. There weren't as many reasons anymore, though. But one good one still remained. When he'd made love to the Josie in his dreams, she'd been a virgin.

The wildest thing east of the Pecos, a virgin? Still, he couldn't shake the image of her on that horse tonight. One with the horse. As confident on a horse as she was with Ivy.

He realized her gaze was still on him, questioning. "I feel as if you cut your ride short because of me. I'm sorry."

She shook her head and looked away. "I was ready to get back."

At least *that* sounded like the truth. He unsaddled the horse and took the saddle into the tack room, which someone had put back in order. He couldn't help wondering what Raymond Degas had been looking for in here.

When he came back out, Josie had put the horses in the corral and stood looking toward the barn on the far side of the stables.

He felt his heart rate jump at the expression on her face. "What?"

"I heard something over by the barn," she whispered, sounding as if she hated to be the one to tell him. Hated that it was happening again. Was it possible she was as confused as he was about all this? "It sounded like it was coming from one of the horse trailers."

"Stay here," he ordered, and took off at a run toward the barn. He was only mildly surprised to hear Josie hot on his heels.

It had to be Raymond, he thought as he slowed beside the barn, wishing he had a weapon. He'd left his pistol locked in his truck, not wanting it around the baby.

He chastised himself for going on the ride. He should have stayed here and watched for Raymond. Except he didn't like letting Josie out of his sight. Because he couldn't trust her. A lie. Because he was worried about her.

That little bit of honesty concerned him. He was letting a woman, who was more than likely a jewel thief—at the least, an accomplice—distract him from what he had to do.

At the horse trailers, he turned to look back at Josie. She had an anxious, worried look on her face that made him wonder if she wanted to talk to Raymond as badly as he did. Maybe more. With Odell dead, Raymond might be the only one who knew where the jewels were. Or he might be the only one alive who could implicate her in the jewel robbery. Blackness bathed this side of the barn, making the horse trailers barely distinguishable. Clay followed the faint rustling sound. Was someone searching one of the horse trailers? It wasn't until he was so close he could touch it, that he saw which trailer it was. Josie's. The one she'd taken when she left Texas.

He'd known she was gone for good when he'd heard she'd taken not only her clothes but her truck, horse, horse trailer and tack.

The consequences of Raymond banging around in her horse trailer only further fueled his suspicions. He glanced back at her, telling himself he'd be a fool to turn his back on this woman for long.

He had that ''I told you so'' look on his face, the one that infuriated her so. Was it now her fault that someone was in her horse trailer? She felt sick inside. First the man in the pines. Then someone in the tack room. Now her horse trailer. Why? And who was it? Raymond Degas?

But what worried her most was the look in Clay's eyes when he'd come riding in a few minutes ago. He'd looked as if he'd seen a ghost. As if she'd done something to make him more suspicious of her.

She followed him now, keeping close, hoping against all hope that he was wrong. That whoever was rummaging around in the trailer wasn't Raymond. Wasn't anyone she knew. Didn't have anything to do with the jewel robbery or Texas or Odell or the past. And especially had nothing to do with her.

But she knew it was too much to hope for.

Clay motioned for her to keep back, his expression threatening. She nodded grudgingly and moved back some as he approached the trailer's side door. Her boot toe stubbed something solid and metallic in the tall grass. She bent down to pick up a foot-long piece of galvanized pipe. A weapon.

This time, no matter who came out of that trailer, she planned to be ready. She wasn't going to have Clay say she'd helped the culprit get away. Not again.

He'd reached the side door to the trailer. She watched him grasp the door handle. So sure of himself, so confident that this time he'd catch Raymond. And catch her as well.

She edged back when he wasn't looking, slinking into the darkness behind the trailer, then working her way around to the other side.

Her horse trailer was old with a stall in the back and an antiquated camper of sorts in the front. It had been her father's when he used to show horses. He'd replaced it with newer, fancier ones as his sons took to the road to show the O'Malley Ranch horses. He'd given his old one to her.

It was supposed to be some sort of punishment because she was often at odds with him over any number of things including his methods of horse training. But she loved the old trailer. To her it was a status symbol. She hadn't sold out. She'd held fast, and if an old horse trailer was the price, then it was well worth it.

The only exit other than the locked horse stall door at the back was the door Clay was guarding, but she knew that a person could get out one of the side windows. She also knew she'd left it open to air out the old camper.

From the other side of the trailer came the sound of the door creaking open, followed instantly by hurried movement. Then a cry of surprise, trailed by a loud oath.

She had the pipe raised and ready when the intruder came flying through the torn window screen. She swung on pure instinct, but fortunately missed as a large raccoon took off across the pasture.

A laugh escaped as she dropped the pipe, relieved tension rushing out of her like air from a busted balloon. But as Clay came around the side of the trailer and she caught the embarrassed expression on his face in the yard light, she burst out laughing.

"Raymond got away again," she said between hiccups of laughter. "Only this time I think he was wearing a mask."

"Very funny," he said, dusting at cobwebs on his jeans. "You're in trouble and you and I know it. Sooner or later it's going to come home to roost. Maybe it already has." He turned and started up the hillside without looking back.

She took a deep breath, the truth of his words stilling the laughter. But she couldn't help smiling at the memory of the raccoon flying out the window—and the look on Clay's face.

Her smile faded at the sudden memory of another face. This one staring out of a stand of pines. Watching her and Ivy.

Clay was right. Except her troubles had *already* come home to roost. When he'd blown into town, bringing with him her past mistakes.

The problem was, she didn't know yet what to do about it.

Chapter Seven

The breeze made the tall grass ripple like water in the moonlight. She could see Clay's broad back ahead of her. His strides long. Angry. His head down, thoughtful.

Thoughtful worried her.

She felt a pang of guilt when she remembered him today with Ivy. When she thought about him watching her work with the horses. Surprise went without saying. But almost admiration. As if he were finally seeing her. Why now of all times?

She shook off the memories. Her days of mooning over Clay Jackson were long behind her. No more daydreaming about what could have been. She knew where she stood with him. And things between them could only get worse.

She quickened her step, anxious to get back to the cabin. She never thought of it as home, even after this long. Home was Texas.

As she neared the cabin, she saw that Mildred

and Ivy hadn't returned from the neighbor's yet. The realization gave her a start until she noticed that it was still early.

But a nugget of fear lodged itself in her stomach. Who else had blown into town along with Raymond and Clay on this ill wind?

Clay had stopped and now stood by the porch, waiting.

"Thanks for walking me home," she said, breezing past him to mount the steps to the porch. She hoped that was subtle enough. She wanted to be alone. She needed desperately to think, and with Clay so near, he made it impossible.

He said nothing. Nor did he move as she crossed the porch and opened the front door.

As she stepped into the cabin, she started to reach for the light switch and stopped, sensing something different, something wrong.

Clay must have seen her hesitation. He was up on the porch in two strides and at her side, gently drawing her hand away from the light switch.

In a shaft of moonlight that sliced in through the window, she could see that the room had been ransacked. Her only thought was: Thank God Mildred has taken Ivy to the neighbor's.

"Stay here," he whispered next to her ear.

He brushed past her, stepping through that wedge of moonlight to disappear into the shadowed darkness of the cabin. Behind her, she could feel the cooler night air coming in through the still-open door.

She saw Clay move, a dark shadow, large and ominous, toward the back of the cabin. But the noise she heard came from upstairs. A rustling sound. Like the one she'd heard the night before in the stables. Her heart leapt into her throat. Raymond?

Clay must have heard it, too. She saw him start up the open stairs at the left of the living room. He moved quietly, cautiously. Although unarmed, he could be as powerful and deadly as a large mountain cat, she recalled, remembering his fight with Odell that day in his stables.

Unable to stand by idly, no matter what he'd said, she slipped across the living room to where she kept a can of pepper spray. Perfect for the stray grizzly she might meet on horseback. Perfect for the stray thief ransacking her cabin.

Quietly, she retraced her steps, going back out the front door into the night, across the porch and down the steps. There were two ways out of the cabin. Through the front door. Or off the second-floor deck. She didn't think whoever was in the cabin would get past Clay this time to go out the front door. That meant the intruder would go for the deck and the stairs that dropped down into the pines below.

She couldn't keep hoping it wasn't Raymond.

This wasn't some random thief here to steal a little horse tack or a few dollars off her bureau.

A cloud cloaked the moon, leaving the sky black as she made her way around the outside of the cabin. The pines stood at the back, the needles even darker than the night. The shadows under them, black as holes and colder.

Josie thought of the face she'd seen looking out of the pine branches across the pasture two evenings ago. Could it have been Raymond? He and Odell *did* look a little alike. Both dark, both tall, but Raymond was definitely not handsome. Maybe the waning light in the pines had played a trick on her. Or just seeing Raymond reminded her of Odell, since they'd been inseparable—except in death, she thought.

The rich smell of pine permeated the late-spring night behind the cabin. She moved to the bottom of the steep stairs that came straight down from the deck.

Carefully, she positioned herself in the trees opposite the last step, suddenly afraid. From this spot, she would see anyone who came down the stairs.

The thought of seeing Raymond Degas again chilled her more than the cool Montana night air. She clutched the pepper spray and waited.

A thud resonated on the second story. Suddenly, the back door slammed open and footfalls hammered across the weathered deck above her, then thudded loudly as they descended the plank steps. Right toward her.

Finally, she'd know the truth. If this man was Raymond. If what she'd feared most was actually coming true.

Another set of boots hit the deck overhead. Clay? He'd never be able to catch whoever was now almost to the bottom.

She held her breath, the pepper spray clutched in her hands, aimed man-high. The moon broke free of the clouds, dappling the deck stairs with silver, distorting the dark shape coming toward her.

He dropped down the last stairs in a flurry of movement. Half running, half falling, hitting the bottom step and stumbling forward—right to her.

It happened so fast. As he fought to get his feet under him, he looked up as if sensing her there. The moonlight fell over his features. Or what would have been his features. A black ski mask flattened his face, making it unrecognizable, monsterlike. Especially the slice of red pressed against the thin slit for his mouth and two marble-size holes for his eyes.

Her finger twitched on the pepper spray trigger.

In that microsecond, their eyes met. His dark and cold and familiar behind the mask. Her heart leapt to her throat, choking back the cry on her lips. He reached out to catch himself. Reached out toward her.

Something glittered in the moonlight. The ring on his right hand. He grabbed the limb right in front of her, the ring just inches from her face.

She fell back against the tree trunk, banging her head. He caught himself on the branch over her head.

Then he was gone, enveloped by the blackness in the pines. Disappearing as if he'd never been there at all.

Before she could take a breath, Clay clambered down the steps, sliding to a surprised stop at the sight of her.

She said nothing, just stared at him, the pepper spray still in her hands. In the distance, an engine turned over. A vehicle sped off into the night.

He swore as he took the pepper spray from her hands, sniffed the nozzle, then tossed it aside. Grabbing her upper arms, he jerked her from the tree branches.

"You saw him?" He sounded angry and frustrated, his tone accusing. "He must have come right past you, so close you couldn't have missed. Why didn't you spray him?"

She looked up at Clay. The moonlight played across his face but couldn't soften the hard lines of his jaw. Nor lighten two-days' growth of stubble. He'd lost his hat. His black hair shone, a raven's wing tumbling over his forehead. She'd never known a more handsome man.

She had the strangest urge to push herself up on tiptoes and kiss him. To lose herself in his kiss. She yearned to be wrapped in his strong arms. To be safe. To be reassured. To be protected.

But the urge lasted only an instant. There'd be no safety in Clay's arms. No reassurance in his kiss. He hadn't come to Montana to protect her. He'd come to catch a thief. Or two. There was no doubt he thought she'd been one of them.

She looked into his eyes and shivered at the cold, searching darkness she found there. Why did he mistrust her so? And how much would he hate her when he finally learned the truth?

"You could have stopped him," Clay said, his words pelting her like hailstones. "You let Raymond get away. Why?"

She looked away, toward the darkness behind the cabin. Toward the darkness of her past. Her mind felt as numb as her body. Every fear she'd ever had—and some she hadn't even dreamed of—seemed to be coming true.

Clay shook her gently as if to bring her back.

She turned her head to look at him again in the silver web of moonlight that sifted down through the tree limbs.

"It wasn't Raymond," she said, her voice

hoarse from the tears that now threatened to close her throat.

He let go of her, stepping back, his gaze hard, unforgiving, unbelieving, reminding her of the last time he'd looked at her like that in Texas. "What do you mean it wasn't Raymond?"

What *did* she mean? Who had she seen? Her mind refused to let her voice her fear. To say it might make it true.

"He wore a mask," she whispered. And a ring—one she'd seen before.

He pulled her closer, his fingers still locked around her slim upper arms. "A mask? What kind of mask?"

"A black ski mask." The moonlight shone on her face, making her appear even paler, her eyes the light-glazed silvery blue of a sleepwalker.

He wanted to shake the truth out of her, but the tremor he felt in her limbs and the lost look in her eyes stopped him. What had she seen tonight that had terrified her so?

More than a masked man coming out of her cabin. He'd stake money on that.

Was it possible that she really didn't know what was going on? Was that why she was so frightened?

He knew that's what he wanted to believe. That Josie had nothing to hide.

Unfortunately, not even his weakening resolve

to nail her to the wall for the jewel theft could make him believe that.

"If there's some reason you're protecting Raymond—"

She seemed to snap out of her trance. Her gaze flew up to his. "The only person I'm protecting is my daughter. Ivy is my *only* concern."

He felt a shock run through him as he looked into her face and saw something that chilled him. The incredible intensity of a mother's love for her child and a desperate need to protect her daughter. Josie would do anything to protect Ivy. *Anything.* Maybe she already had.

"Look, I didn't mean—"

"You have no idea what we've been through," she snapped angrily. "What we still have to get through." Her eyes glistened shiny with anger and tears. "Don't you think I know my daughter's in danger? What you don't seem to realize is that Ivy's been in danger from the moment she was conceived."

He stared at her. "What do you mean?"

"Odell." She looked away. "He threatened to…hurt her if I went through with the pregnancy."

Clay felt fury burn through him like flames. He wanted to kill Odell and wished he wasn't dead so he could. He looked over the top of her head to the dark pines, feeling like he might explode. It was a good thing Odell was dead. But his best friend Raymond was still alive.

He barely heard the sound of a vehicle coming up the road to the cabin. Mildred bringing Ivy home?

His gaze dropped to Josie's face. It shone in the moonlight, raw with fear. He felt his heart break at the thought of her alone and afraid and pregnant.

"You're right." He hesitated to let her go, as if he might break his only connection to her, a tenuous connection at best. "I don't know what you and Ivy have been through. I only wish you'd have come to me when Odell threatened you." Come to me before that. Beside the creek. "I'm sorry."

Her eyes filled with tears as she looked up at him.

He let her go, fighting the conflicting emotions his heart pumped through him. "I have to leave for a while. Can you ask Mildred to stay with you and Ivy until I get back?"

She nodded.

"Are you going to be all right?" he asked.

She squared her shoulders, brushing her knuckles across her cheek at the escaping tears. "Yes."

He picked up the pepper spray from where he'd tossed it and handed it to her. "I have to go," he repeated, as if she gave a damn. Actually, she'd probably love it if he left and never came back. *No such luck, Josie.*

But he had to find Raymond. Had to get to the truth. Now more than ever before. He knew damned well that he'd tailed Raymond from Texas to the Buffalo Jump Ranch—and Josie. Now he just wanted to know why. He wanted to hear Raymond say it.

He'd been wrong about so much. He wanted desperately to be wrong about Josie. But he knew this *had* to be about the jewels. There wasn't any other explanation. Too much money was involved. Too many people. If it really hadn't been Raymond who'd ransacked Josie's cabin, then someone else was also looking for the jewels. He didn't like the feeling that he was the only one who didn't know the score. And Josie O'Malley was right smack in the middle of it all.

"I'll be back," he said as he started across the field to where he'd left his pickup.

She didn't acknowledge that she'd heard him. Not that it mattered. He'd be back, anyway. Hopefully with some answers from Raymond Degas. But he'd be back. One way or the other. Because he wasn't finished with Josie. Only now he wanted to prove her innocence. If he could.

JOSIE ACTUALLY DID as he'd suggested. She knew she had to do something. She couldn't just keep hoping he was wrong. Not after what had happened the past two nights.

Just the thought of the masked man who'd come flying off her deck chilled her to the bone. Who had he been? She refused to let her mind even speculate—let alone taunt her with the one possibility she couldn't accept. Not yet.

But she also could no longer pretend this would all blow over. She hugged herself, trying to get warm, as she went to meet Mildred.

"How was Ivy?" she asked, smiling at the sight of her daughter's tiny sleeping form in the back of the car as Mildred opened her door and the dome light came on.

"A bit tuckered out," Mildred said. "Me, too. But she has so much fun with Rachel. I didn't let her eat too much cake or ice cream, though."

"I'm sure you didn't." Josie bit back the tears that threatened. What would she have done without Mildred and Ruth?

"What is it, Josie?" Mildred asked now with concern as Josie got her daughter from the car seat.

"The cabin's kind of a mess," she answered as they climbed up to the porch, Josie carrying the sleeping Ivy in her arms. The front door still stood open.

"Oh, my," Mildred exclaimed when she saw the ransacked interior. "Was it the same person who was in the tack room?"

"Probably," Josie fibbed, not wanting to upset Mildred more. "I wish I could tell you what's going on. Clay still thinks someone is looking for missing jewels from a robbery in Texas." She headed up the stairs with Mildred behind her carrying Ivy's things.

"What do you think?" Mildred asked as she helped her slip off Ivy's party clothes and dress the toddler for bed.

"I don't know why anyone would think the jewels were here."

She tucked the blanket around Ivy and leaned down to kiss her again, loving the warm, baby-soft feel of her. Ivy smiled in her sleep and let out a tiny sigh. Josie smiled down at her through her tears and made a silent prayer.

"Are you afraid this might have something to do with Ivy's father?" Mildred asked.

She looked up in surprise. Mildred had no idea how close she'd come to the truth. "Yes."

"Where is Mr. Jackson?" Mildred asked accusingly.

She checked the baby intercom system Ruth had given her, then the locks on the windows and the back door before she headed down the stairs again. "He had to go into town."

"That's it, I'm calling my friend Charley Brainard," Mildred said, going to the living room phone. "Now, don't you argue."

Josie wasn't about to argue. In fact, she'd just been about to suggest that Mildred call Charley to come stay with them for a while.

Charley Brainard was a huge, likable man, who from what Josie could tell, had quite the crush on Mildred. "I think having Charley come over is a great idea." In more ways than Mildred could imagine. "I need to go into town, and I want to be sure that you and Ivy are safe while I'm gone."

Ten minutes later, Charley drove up the road. By then, she and Mildred had tidied up the cabin, all evidence of the intruder gone but certainly not forgotten.

Mildred went to get Charley a tall lemonade.

"Please don't let anyone in," she said to Charley while Mildred was still in the kitchen. "Anyone at all. You can hear Ivy on the intercom." Or anyone else who might break into the house.

"Don't you worry about that little darling of yours," Charley assured her. "Or Mildred, either. I'll take good care of them."

"I know you will. I left the pepper spray on the top shelf, just in case. I won't be long."

"You just take care of yourself," Mildred said, coming in with Charley's lemonade.

Although she knew Ivy would be safer with Charley and Mildred than alone with her, she still had a hard time leaving. But she had to find Raymond. Had to find out what he was doing in Montana. What he'd been doing in her stables. And who had ransacked her cabin tonight.

She had to be wrong. There had to be another explanation. Other than the one that had a death grip on her.

Chapter Eight

Josie took the short way to town, hoping to avoid running into Clay. She figured he'd go looking for Raymond with the same intentions she had. Or at least close.

But if Raymond was in Three Forks, she knew she'd be able to find him. Hopefully before Clay.

She took the old road, fighting hard not to panic. There had to be an explanation. For everything that was happening. For what she thought she'd seen tonight. *Who* she thought she'd seen.

At a phone booth just outside of town, she stopped, dug some quarters out of her purse and called what few motels there were, asking for a Texan driving a Lincoln Continental, pretending she'd run into his car and was trying to find the owner. The Lincoln had Texas plates and she'd seen a cowboy in it earlier, but she didn't know the driver's name.

She came up empty in town, where someone like

Raymond would have stuck out like a sore thumb. But she wasn't surprised that he'd opted not to stay in Three Forks. He and his Lincoln would be too visible.

And by now he had to know that Clay Jackson was after him. Maybe not just Clay, she thought, remembering the man who'd ransacked her cabin. More people than just Clay might be looking for Raymond.

Because of that, she figured Raymond would hole up. Or take off.

She was betting he'd stuck around, though, and that worried her even more. Raymond wasn't what she'd ever considered a brave man. Nor was he stupid. With this much heat on him, he *should* have run.

If he hadn't, then, Josie wondered why. What was he waiting for? What was he in town looking for? The jewels from the robbery, as Clay suspected? Or something else?

She tried the motels in the surrounding small towns. No luck. Maybe he was camping out somewhere near town. That would make him almost impossible to find, given the number of campgrounds in the area.

Running out of ideas and thinking she'd have to give up, at least for tonight, she remembered the motel up on the interstate. Fort Three Forks.

Maybe Raymond would have seen some irony in staying at a fort. Odell would have.

She pocketed the rest of her change and decided to drive out rather than call.

The night had cleared, leaving a full moon and a billion tiny stars to reflect on the water as she crossed the Jefferson River.

As she neared the Fort Three Forks motel, she glanced across the highway at the Steer Inn, hoping to see the Lincoln. Raymond would have to eat. He'd go for a Montana beef steak, probably chicken-fried, just as Odell would have. Odell. She turned up the heater in the truck, feeling chilled, but not from the night.

No Lincoln at the Steer Inn. Nor parked in front of Fort Three Forks. She pulled around back and looked between the motor homes, hoping she'd get lucky.

Discouraged, she backed up and swung around to leave. Her headlights picked up the shine of a chrome bumper across an expanse of asphalt. She swung the pickup's lights around again, illuminating the white of Texas plates.

The dented, rusted, cream-colored Lincoln she'd seen Clay watching just two nights before sat on the dark side of a large metal building a hundred yards away. In her headlights she could see that the side window on the passenger side was a quarter of the way down, the front left tire looking a little low on air, the windshield cracked. The car appeared empty.

She parked her pickup, raked a hand through her unruly hair and headed for the motel lobby. Raymond wasn't quite as smart as she'd thought. If she'd found him, anyone else looking for him could have, too.

She opened the motel lobby door and stepped in, as the consequences of that thought sunk in. She hoped she wasn't too late.

Laying on her Texas accent a little thick, she tried to get Raymond's room number, knowing he wouldn't have registered in his own name. She came up with a story about being homesick. That much at least was true. And that she'd seen the Texas plates, realized whoever it was was from her neck of the woods and wanted to take them dinner and hear about home.

The girl behind the desk was sympathetic, but she couldn't give out his room number. She offered to ring his room, though, because she remembered him and his southern accent.

Josie watched her. No answer. The girl suggested she leave a message for him.

Josie took the notepad and wrote ''Call me'' and her number, but she planned to find Raymond before he read it. She'd seen the girl dial room 211.

She thanked her and left, doubling back to take the set of outside stairs up to the open second-floor balcony that ran the length of the rooms. At room 211 she knocked and waited, watching the parking lot behind her over her shoulder.

No answer.

She knocked again. ''Maid,'' she said, hiding the Texan in her accent as much as she could.

Still no answer.

The curtains on the window were closed, but she could see through a crack where the edges didn't quite meet.

She cupped her hands to her face and peered in. The room was dark except for the flicker of the TV screen across the room. It illuminated the only object she could see clearly. The bed. Queen-size. The bright-colored spread hanging off the side, the white sheets crumpled.

She waited, thinking he might have gone into the bathroom. She knew she couldn't wait long. She was too visible up here from both the highway and the parking lot.

But after what seemed like an eternity and Raymond hadn't returned, she looked across the pavement toward the Lincoln, still hunkered away from the lights of the motel in the shadow of the warehouse. Maybe he'd walked across the street to the Steer Inn for dinner.

Her stomach fluttered as she stared at the car, remembering the partially open passenger side window. She would be able to get into the car. See who it was registered to. Or if there was anything inside that would prove Raymond Degas was in Three Forks.

She took the stairs back to the parking lot, trying to convince herself she should wait in her pickup for Raymond to return. But it was getting late and she was anxious to get home to Ivy. She started toward the Lincoln. At least she'd find out if the car was registered to him.

Goose bumps dimpled across her skin as she neared the Lincoln. Just a few days ago she'd been thinking how content she was. She'd actually felt safe, having convinced herself that the past could no longer hurt her. That she could go back to Texas. Soon.

Had she really been that naive?

She reached the dented front fender of the car and looked across the long rusted hood to the windshield. It was too dark to see inside the car even if the windows hadn't been tinted for the Texas heat. She wished she'd brought a flashlight. Even more, a weapon.

Moving down the side of the car toward the partially open side window, she suddenly felt as if she wasn't alone.

No moonlight found this side of the huge warehouse. Nor did starlight. In the distance, cars hummed by on the interstate. Faint laughter rode the breeze over from the motel to echo off the building, leaving a heavy silence. Something moved in the tall grass of the fields off to her left, making her jump. An animal?

Nearer, she thought she heard another sound. Low. Almost a moan. The breeze picked up. She caught a whiff of something. A mixture of mildew, years of road dust and something else, a sharp, coppery smell. Blood.

Her heart drummed, reverberating against her ribs, making her weak and off balance. She stared at the partially open window, but she could see nothing but darkness inside the car.

Run! All her instincts cried for her to turn, run and not look back.

She thought of Ivy and took a step backward, planning to do just that.

But then she heard the moan. A low, pain-filled plea that seemed to hang in the night.

Her pulse thrummed in her ears. The sound *had* come from the car, hadn't it? She glanced off to her left. The lights from the motel and the interstate lit a stretch of open field.

But even before she heard the moan again, she knew it hadn't come from out there.

She stood motionless, her breath caught between her teeth. Only her right arm moved away from her body and toward the car door handle.

It took every ounce of her strength and courage to open the door. The latch clicked, startling her, then the big, heavy door swung out. The dome light flashed on, blinding her for an instant. And the body that had been propped against the door fell out, hitting her legs and sliding to the ground with a heavy thud and a groan.

She let out a startled cry as she recognized the man bleeding at her feet and saw the gun he had pointed at her head.

THREE FORKS WAS DEAD for a Saturday night. Clay had driven past the motel where he'd spotted the Lincoln Continental before, then past the bars and restaurants and gas stations, all without any luck.

The waitress at the Headwaters Café had told him that most tourists wouldn't start rolling in until after Memorial Day. Fly fishermen. Golfers. Families on their way to Yellowstone Park or Lewis and Clark Caverns. A few would want to see where the Missouri began. Most just passing through on their way somewhere else.

That should have made finding Raymond Degas easy. Three Forks wasn't that big. And how many old rusted and dented 1975 cream-colored Lincoln Continentals with Texas plates could there be?

He'd searched the side streets, alleys and driveways of the small town, driving slowly, wondering if he really knew who he was chasing anymore.

Josie had him doubting himself, something he rarely did. Doubts were dangerous for an investigator. When he started questioning his gut feelings, he was in trouble. And as good as dead.

Worse, Josie had him doubting a lot more than his gut instincts. She had him questioning everything. Including whether or not he'd really been on Raymond Degas's trail or someone else's.

Of course the man Clay had been following didn't go by Degas. Or Raymond. He registered under different names and Clay figured the Lincoln was probably borrowed. Or stolen.

But Clay knew a surefire way to prove who the man was. Fingerprints. Degas had had a record since he was a juvie. If Clay could find the Lincoln, he knew he could get a clear print to send to the crime lab in Austin.

He hadn't bothered before because he'd been so sure he had Degas. Now he wasn't sure of anything, especially what had happened two years ago. Concerning the jewel robbery. Concerning Josie.

He kept thinking about her working with the horses in the pen this morning. He'd never seen anyone who was that good with unbroken horses, and he'd seen his share of horse trainers.

Watching her ride tonight like the devil himself was chasing her had left him shaken. Because he'd seen her ride like that before. Only once. On a horse he'd thought no one could ride.

He felt as if he couldn't be sure what was real and what wasn't anymore.

He widened his search to the businesses near the interstate, trying to concentrate on what he *did* know for certain: He'd followed *someone* whom he had reason to believe was Raymond Degas from Texas to Three Forks, Montana. Followed him to the ranch where Josie worked.

Raymond had made it easy, leaving behind a trail any fool could follow.

The thought rattled around in his head like a loose marble. He slowed the pickup, realizing he'd assumed Raymond was a fool. Or that the man no longer thought anyone was looking for him.

But Raymond had disappeared and stayed hidden for almost two years from the cops and Clay who'd been looking for him. That made Raymond no fool. He had to know that the heat hadn't died on the jewels. So what would make him blow his cover? What would make him leave a clearly marked trail for Clay to follow?

His heart began to pound with a vengeance. He swallowed and slowed the truck to a crawl. For *Clay Jackson* to follow. The anonymous tip about Raymond. The easy-to-follow trail. Had Raymond wanted Clay to follow him to Montana? To Josie?

But why?

He drove down the short road to the Fort Three Forks motel. No Lincoln. He pulled around back to check the parking lot. But instead of finding the one vehicle he'd been looking for, he found the one he'd least expected.

Slowly he rolled down his window and parked alongside Josie's pickup. Empty. What the hell was she doing— He never got to finish the thought.

A gunshot shattered the quiet summer night.

CLAY'S GAZE LEAPT up at the sound. Through the darkness and his open side window, he saw the Lincoln parked behind the warehouse in the distance. The passenger side door hung open. The glow from the dome light spilled out onto the pavement, onto what looked like a body. No, more than one body. There appeared to be two figures on the ground.

Josie. That's all he could think. Josie and trouble had always gone together. He grabbed his pistol and jumped out, keeping to the darkness as he ran toward the Lincoln.

He slowed, unsure, as he neared the front of the car. The night glittered, a canopy of stars and a large white moon, but none of that light reached the side of the warehouse. Just that small circle of pale gold stealing out of the Lincoln.

As far as he could tell, neither of the figures on the ground had heard him approach. That surprised—and worried—him.

He slowed at the sound. A hoarse, hurried whisper.

Weapon ready, he edged carefully around the front of the car until he could see behind the door hanging open.

He'd been right. Two figures were beside the car on the ground. The smaller one, a woman, knelt over a man sprawled in a pool of blood. He seemed to be trying to tell the woman something.

Clay stepped closer.

Josie lifted her head at the sound of his approach, her face pale and drawn, shock glittering in her eyes. He couldn't tell if it was from seeing him or what had happened before he got here.

He let out a low curse. What the hell was she doing here?

She brushed a wisp of stray blond hair back, her blue eyes too bright in the car's dome light.

He motioned for to her to move back from the man on the ground. As she got to her feet, he saw the gun beside the body and hoped to hell it wasn't hers. Or that her fingerprints weren't on it. But with Josie, anything was possible.

Then he stepped close enough he could see the man's face.

Up close, it was clear that Raymond Degas *had* changed during the past two years. He was thinner, his hair long and dirty, his face more pockmarked. But there wasn't any doubt that he was the man Clay had followed from Texas or that he was Raymond Degas.

Raymond stared up, his eyes blank and distant. Blood no longer ran from the bullet hole in his chest.

Although he knew it was useless, Clay leaned over him to check for a pulse. None.

"Is he dead?" Josie whispered.

"Yeah," he said, straightening.

She couldn't seem to take her eyes off of the dead man.

Clay assumed the shot had come from the gun lying beside Raymond, but he didn't like to take chances where murder—and this woman—were concerned.

She stared at Raymond for a few moments longer, then looked up, blinking as if she couldn't bring him into focus. She seemed to notice what he still held in his left hand. A loaded .357 Magnum. Her gaze flicked back up to his. "You don't think *I* killed him?"

Nothing about Josie would surprise him at this point. But cold-blooded murder?

As far as he could tell, she wasn't armed. But what had she been thinking coming here? She should have known that Raymond was dangerous. Obviously his associates were even more dangerous.

"What are you doing here?" he demanded, angry with her for risking her life. But even more angry that she'd even gotten involved with someone like Raymond—and Odell—in the first place. "I thought I told you to stay at the cabin with Mildred and Ivy."

She didn't answer, just looked at him blankly.

"The police aren't going to like that answer," he said, reaching into his coat for his cell phone. He watched her chew at her lower lip as he dialed 911.

"Did you see anyone besides Raymond?" he asked while he waited for a ring.

She shook her head and glanced toward the interstate. A string of lights dotted the highway like tiny gold beads.

The 911 operator answered. He relayed the information to the sheriff's department and hung up.

"You didn't see who shot him?" Clay persisted as he led her away from the murder scene to a bench outside the motel.

She sat down. "I didn't see anyone but Raymond, and I didn't even know it was him until he fell out on the ground when I opened the door. He was bleeding, the front of his shirt was soaked." She looked down at her jeans. They had blood on them. "He fell against me."

"Who fired the shot?" Clay asked.

She shook her head. "I guess *he* did."

"Then he had the pistol in his hand when you opened the door?"

"Yes." She closed her eyes. "It happened so fast."

Didn't she realize the cops would grill her a lot worse than this? "Try to remember exactly what happened."

She opened her eyes and looked over at him. "Can't you just leave me alone for a minute?"

What did he have to do to get this woman to tell him what was going on?

"The cops are going to want to know why you came looking for Raymond," he said, losing his temper. "*Someone* murdered him. It's all going to come out. Everything that you thought you'd left behind in Texas is now coming after you. You can't escape it. Can't you see that?"

More than he knew. She felt herself shiver. She looked away. In the distance she could hear the sirens and see a string of flashing red-and-blue lights headed this way.

Clay was right about one thing. She needed help. She could no longer pretend that she could handle this alone. Not after finding Raymond the way she had. Not after what he'd whispered to her.

"I want to help you, Josie," Clay said softly, urgently. "I know you're in trouble, and it's getting worse. I heard Raymond tell you something. You have to trust someone. Why not me, Josie?"

Something in his voice tugged at her heartstrings. Tears rushed her eyes, her throat closing over the lump lodged there.

She pushed up off the bench and walked a few feet away, her back to him. She didn't want him to see her tears. Nor could she face him right now.

Why not Clay Jackson? At one time she could have thought of a half-dozen reasons. But right now, she could think of only one. But didn't that make him the last man she should trust with this?

She turned to look back at him, knowing she had little other choice. He wouldn't give up. Eventually he'd find out everything.

She only wished she could have trusted him with the truth in Texas. How different would things have turned out?

"The man who ransacked my cabin, the one I saw coming down the deck stairs—" She could hear the sheriff's department sirens coming nearer. They would be here soon. She dreaded facing the cops, but not more than she did Clay's reaction to what she had to tell him.

She thought of the fear she'd seen in Raymond's eyes. They now shared a common enemy. She had to tell Clay. Warn him.

He seemed to brace himself. She just hoped he could take the truth, because this was only the beginning and she feared it was going to get a whole lot worse.

"It was Odell Burton."

Chapter Nine

Clay stared at her as the sheriff's cars screamed around the turn headed for them, lights flashing, sirens blaring.

"Odell? Odell's dead," he said, as if he had to remind her.

She said nothing.

"You couldn't have seen Odell. It was dark and…" He focused on her. "You said he wore a mask."

"It *was* dark," she admitted. "And he *did* wear a mask, but I saw his eyes and he was wearing his class ring." She looked up, expecting to see the same doubt on his face that she'd heard in his voice. The same doubts she'd had herself. Until she'd found Raymond shot and dying.

Clay was frowning, his brows furrowed, his gaze hard. She *thought* he might remember that ring. It had left a tiny scar at Clay's hairline after Odell had blindsided him in the stables two years ago.

Few people knew about the scar because it was hidden by Clay's hair. But *she* knew it was there because she'd been the reason Odell had hit him. The tiny scar was a reminder for her of the mistakes she'd made with not one man but two.

Clay said nothing. Couldn't think of anything to say. He remembered that ring, all right. Just as well as he did Odell's lazy, arrogant smile. It had been the smile of a man who had something Clay wanted. Josie.

The assault of memories dug up dark and ugly reminders. Odell was dead. Clay had been at the morgue when Odell's father came in to identify Odell's effects. The ring had been one of them.

"Do you know how many class rings like Odell's there are in the world?" He shook his head and looked away from Josie to the group of uniformed men approaching fast. She was mistaken.

But he couldn't shake the memory of her at the bottom of the deck stairs, her fingers locked on the can of pepper spray, her eyes filled with shock. And terror.

"I know you've never taken my advice in the past," he said under his breath. "But I wouldn't mention this to the cops. At least not yet."

She shot him a look that clearly said "What? The let's-be-honest Clay Jackson suggesting she lie?"

"But of course you'll do as you please. You

always have," he added, then stepped forward to introduce himself to the Gallatin County sheriff's deputy.

FOR THE NEXT COUPLE of hours, Clay found himself lost in the surreal activity around the Lincoln. Cop-car lights flashing. Camera bulbs going off. Questions and more questions. The scream of sirens as the coroner arrived. Then the ambulance.

A crowd had gathered and stood barricaded back by the motel. Clay took it all in, never letting Josie out of his sight. Or out of earshot if he could help it.

The instant he'd gotten the chance, he called Judge Branson in San Antonio and, cashing in an old debt, asked the judge to have Odell Burton's body exhumed immediately. Judge Branson wasn't happy about being awakened in the middle of the night, let alone about the urgent request, but he'd grudgingly agreed to do it.

"You'd better be right about this, Clay," he'd said just before he hung up.

Clay would be quite happy to hear that he was wrong. That Odell Burton was six feet under and had been for almost two years. Then maybe both he and Josie could put the man to rest.

"I really need to get back to my daughter," he heard her tell the deputy in charge.

"I understand," the officer said. "Just a couple

more questions. Why were you looking for Mr. Degas?''

''I thought I saw him on two occasions at the ranch where I work, the Buffalo Jump Ranch.''

''I know Ruth Slocum well,'' the deputy said, nodding and smiling.

''Both times I didn't get a chance to talk to him,'' Josie continued. ''I thought maybe Raymond had some news from my family.''

''You're from Texas, right?''

As if her accent wasn't a dead giveaway.

''The hill country. My family still lives around San Antonio.''

The deputy nodded and scribbled in his notebook. ''Neither of you is planning to leave town, right?'' he asked, looking up at Clay.

''No,'' Clay assured him. He wasn't leaving until he got the truth out of Josie, and God only knew how long that would take.

''I'm not going anywhere,'' she said, but she had that wild look in her eyes again like a horse about to take off over the next hill.

Clay put his arm around her shoulders as he walked her to her pickup.

''You didn't tell him about the break-ins—or about Odell,'' he said. ''I'm not used to you taking my advice. Are you all right?''

They'd reached her pickup, but she didn't want the warmth and weight of his arm and fingers to leave her shoulders. Not yet. It had been too long since she'd felt the weight of a man's arm around her.

She didn't move for a few moments, didn't even look at him for fear he'd see how much she needed him. It didn't matter that she had no right.

"I'm serious," he said quietly. "Are you all right?"

She glanced toward the Lincoln. The ambulance had taken Raymond's body away, but uniformed men still swarmed the area around it. Looking for a murderer.

The night had turned darker, colder. The landscape more lonely. More malevolent. She felt spooked, on edge, nervous. But why wouldn't she? She'd just seen a dead man for the second time today.

She reached into her pocket to dig for her keys. He took his arm back. She could feel his gaze searching her face. She didn't look at him. Couldn't look at him.

Her fingers closed over her keys. She couldn't keep running. Not from the truth. Not from Clay.

"No, I'm not all right," she said, surprising herself. She looked up at him.

A chill seemed to move through her like a restless spirit. Odell. Dead or alive, he and Raymond had brought Clay back into her life. "I know who killed Raymond,'' she said, her throat hoarse with unshed tears. ''He told me.''

Clay's jaw dropped. ''You aren't going to say—''

''Odell. It was the last thing Raymond said. 'Odell did it.''' Her voice broke. ''He's alive, and I'm scared to death that he'll come for me and Ivy next.''

He'd been afraid that was what she was going to say.

''Why, Josie? I can understand that Odell didn't want you to have the baby because he didn't want to be responsible for it, but why would he want to hurt the two of you now? Even if he *were* alive, that doesn't make any sense.''

He watched her look again at the Lincoln, her eyes filled with terror, but she said nothing.

''I can help you,'' he pressed. ''What is it I did that you think you can't trust me?''

Her gaze jerked back to him.

He looked into the blue depths of her eyes, trying to understand the sadness, the regret. Was it more than getting involved with Odell? More than her fear of the man?

''I have to tell you what happened two years ago,'' she said, her voice soft as the night breeze.

He felt a jolt. A flash of memory that filled him with fear.

''But I need to be sure Ivy is all right first,'' she

said. She'd already called the cabin. All three times, Mildred had assured her that Ivy was fine. "I need to hold her, Clay."

Clay. Not Jackson. He reached over and took Josie's keys from her hand. "I'll take you home."

HE DROVE TOWARD the ranch, the moon high, the night dark. His head hurt. Too much had happened tonight. Too much remained unresolved. Thoughts flashed in and out like signs caught along the road in the headlights.

Why did Josie have reason to fear Odell? There wasn't any way Odell could have survived the car accident. He'd seen the demolished, burned-out car. He'd also seen Odell's remains at the morgue.

No, Josie was wrong. Odell Burton was dead. But why was she so afraid he wasn't?

They rode in silence, his gaze on the narrow road ahead. Josie's staring out into the darkness.

The sandstone bluffs of the old buffalo jump shone pale tan in the moonlight, making them appear closer as he turned off the paved two-lane highway and onto the gravel road that ran to the ranch. The headlights cut a path through the darkness along the river, making the night seem more empty and the two of them more alone.

Josie looked exhausted, her face ghostly in the jade glow from the dash lights. She let out a long sigh and looked over at him. "I hated Odell."

He raised a brow.

"I've always hated Odell," she said, spitting out the words.

He almost drove in the ditch. "Then why in God's name did you...date him?"

"Date him?" she asked, narrowing her gaze as she glared over at him. "You were the one who thought I was dating him. The truth is, the more I rejected him, the more obsessed he became with having me."

It took him a moment to let that sink in. "But I saw you kissing him—"

"You saw *him* kissing me, and he only did it to get a rise out of you, and it worked," she said, disgusted. "Odell thought you wanted me and he couldn't bear it. Everything with Odell was about winning and losing. He hated to lose. Refused to lose."

He drove in silence the last couple of miles, his hands gripping the wheel, his heart pounding. He didn't dare speak for fear of what he'd say.

He parked between Mildred's car and a pickup he didn't recognize but that he assumed belonged to the Charley Josie had told him about. A single light glowed inside the cabin. Mildred waved from the front window. He saw the relief on Josie's face, heard her breathe a sigh as she got out of the truck and headed for the cabin.

He followed her, feeling shell-shocked. How

long had he believed that Josie had feelings for Odell? Or at least that she'd dated Odell because he was wild and dangerous and she was rebelling against her family—and against Clay himself.

But if that hadn't been the case— It made him more than doubt himself. If he'd been this wrong about Josie and Odell, could he be wrong about everything else? But Josie had gotten pregnant with Odell's child. How did she explain that?

He followed Josie into the cabin and thanked Mildred and Charley for watching Ivy while she went up to see her daughter. "I'll take care of them now."

Mildred introduced him to Charley and seemed to hesitate. She studied him, obviously sizing him up.

"I'm worried about Josie," she said.

"Me, too." He walked Mildred and Charley out to their cars. She opened the door of her Honda but stopped short of getting in.

"Josie told me that the father of her baby wasn't good for her or Ivy and that's why she left Texas, left him." Her gaze locked on him in the light coming from the car. "You seem to care for her and Ivy." She waited as if needing an answer.

"More than you know."

She nodded, her expression stern. "Whatever happened in Texas, it's not too late to make it up to her."

"I hope you're right about that."

Without another word, she got into the car and closed the door. As she pulled out, Charley fell in behind her. The two vehicles disappeared down the road.

Clay turned back to the cabin. He found Josie sitting upstairs next to the crib in an antique oak rocker, her gaze on her sleeping toddler. He couldn't remember Josie ever looking more appealing. Her love for her daughter shone in her eyes and seemed to soften and illuminate her face, making her all the more beautiful.

But he could see the exhaustion in the slope of her shoulders, in the deep blue reaches of her eyes, in the desperation he glimpsed there.

"Come on," he said softly. "Let's get you to bed."

She looked up at him, not appearing surprised to see him. "Clay."

She made it sound like an endearment, her voice soft, breathy. He could get used to her calling him that instead of Jackson.

"I need to tell you the rest."

He nodded. "But not tonight, Josie. In the morning will be soon enough. We can talk then. You need to get some rest."

"You're staying?" she asked, sounding hopeful.

He smiled. "I'll be on the couch if you need me. Don't worry."

"Thank you." Her gaze met his and held it as tenderly as an embrace.

He felt a shock of current run between them. He cupped her cheek in his palm. Her skin felt warm and soft, her gaze almost inviting. He bent closer. She tilted her face up, an open invitation.

His lips grazed hers. Lightly. He wanted to devour her, to taste and probe and take and give back. But he kissed her gently, their breaths mingling.

Her hand suddenly clutched his shoulder. Her fingers dug in as she pulled him down to her. She deepened the kiss, her mouth hot and wet and demanding.

A flash of memory raced through him, teasing his senses. Taunting him. She had kissed him like this before. Not by her barn. But by the creek. In the flickering campfire light. In the dream.

He pulled her into his arms, shoving away the fantasy of Josie for the real thing. Only this moment mattered. Only the feel of her lips. The promise in her eyes. Both so strong he felt empowered, as if this had always been their destiny and nothing on earth could stop it.

Passion, as hot and bright as sunlight, filled him. Heat sizzled over his skin. He lost himself in her eyes, her lips, her taste, her touch, the incredible erotic scent of her. He'd never wanted her more than he did now.

She tugged at his shirt, pulling the tail from his

jeans, then ran her hands up under it over his chest. Her cool touch ignited his flesh as her fingertips skimmed over him like a chill.

In the haze of desire, he looked down at her. He saw his own desire reflected in her eyes.

She moaned softly. "Please."

All reason escaped him as she pressed her lips to his, her body, soft and full and ripe, against his.

He swept her up into his arms and headed across the hall to her bedroom. She looped her arms around his neck, her gaze locked on his. He shoved open the door and strode to the bed. As he carefully laid her down, she pulled him on top of her, pulled him into a kiss.

He could think of nothing but her now, his need for her, her need for him as they both struggled to rid themselves of each other's clothing.

Fumbling, he unbuttoned her shirt, drawing it back to reveal the plain white bra against her lightly freckled skin. So prim. So proper. So virginal. The thought shocked him, jarring a memory as he slipped one strap from her shoulder. Then the other. Then peeled away the bra.

Her breasts swelled. Her nipples, hard nubs against his palm.

He bent to suck at her breast. Josie groaned and cradled his face in her hands.

"Clay, oh, Clay."

She pulled away the rest of his clothing and he slowly drew down her panties.

Now, his hardness against her softness, bare skin against bare skin, they locked their arms around each other, bodies melding together with heat and longing.

Josie heard Ivy's cry first. She pulled her lips back from his, her eyes molten steel. "It's Ivy," she whispered. "She's probably wet."

They both listened to see if the toddler would fall back to sleep. The cries grew louder.

"Let me," he said, getting out of bed to pull on his jeans.

"Are you sure?" she asked.

He nodded and grinned. "I'll be right back."

He padded into Ivy's bedroom and turned on the light. "What seems to be the problem, little one?" he asked as he leaned over the crib. She was sitting in the middle of the crib, tears in her big brown eyes.

She smiled when she saw him and babbled something he didn't understand.

He wiped her tears, then checked her diaper. Wet. Just as Josie had suspected.

He laid her down, unfastened the wet diaper, glad to see it was nothing more than that, and applied the moisturized wipe, then slid another diaper under the wriggling toddler.

Ivy giggled and babbled away, kicking her legs

and waving her arms and trying to get up, as he tried a half dozen times to figure out how the disposable diapers attached.

Finally, he succeeded and pulled the blanket over Ivy. She had settled back down, her dark eyes flickering closed as he leaned down to plant a kiss on her forehead. What an adorable kid, he thought as he turned out the light and started to leave.

He stopped at the door, glancing back. In the dim light of the night-light he saw Ivy's eyes close. He waited for a few more seconds but she didn't open them again.

He tiptoed back to Josie's bedroom. In the dark, he could see her lying on the bed. But as he neared, he heard the steady, rhythmic breathing.

"Josie?"

She didn't stir.

He stared down at her. As angelic as her daughter. He pulled the blanket up to her chin, covering her delectable naked body and holding his desire at bay. When she still hadn't stirred, he picked up his clothing and headed downstairs to the couch.

Several hours later, shivering and aching for just the nearness of her, he returned upstairs, stripped off his jeans and climbed in beside her. She snuggled against him, sighing softly.

He smiled and closed his eyes, at peace.

MORNING BROKE BRIGHT and sunny. Josie stirred and rolled over, seeking the wondrous heat that enveloped her as she'd slept. But the bed was cold and empty. Just as it had always been. She felt an odd desolation, missing something she'd never had. Or had she last night?

She lay on her back, watching the sun play on the ceiling, wishing she could get back the feeling she'd had before opening her eyes. With only a faint memory of the dream to keep her warm, she clung to it, unable to remember anything more than a feeling of being cherished in a cocoon of heat and safety.

Closing her eyes, she tried to remember more, but it was gone. Just like the darkness.

Her eyes flew open at the sound of voices in Ivy's bedroom across the hall. Had Mildred spent the night? Josie tried to remember what had happened last night but couldn't discern reality from dreamland.

Ivy's sweet laugh floated into the bedroom and Josie smiled, some of the warmth coming back. Then she heard another voice. Definitely not Mildred's. She threw back the covers, shocked to find herself naked, her skin flushed.

She stood, the cool morning air raising goose bumps across her flesh as the sound of Clay's voice washed her with heat. She reached for her robe, an uneasy feeling settling in the pit of her stomach.

Last night: Raymond. Murder. Clay. Cops.

Cabin. Kiss. Nothing after that but warmth and fuzziness.

She tied her robe around her and moved toward the sound of Ivy's and Clay's laughter. It filled the cabin, as sweet and pure as sunlight, and tugged unmercifully at her heart. The cabin had needed the sound of male laughter. Until that moment, she hadn't realized how much.

Clay's deep, soft voice stopped her at the doorway to Ivy's room. "About this diaper," he was saying as he leaned over her daughter, his large strong hands fumbling with the tabs. His voice as soft and gentle as his movements. "It's a lot easier to put on with a little cooperation from you. You know what I mean?"

Ivy giggled and kicked vigorously, making Clay laugh.

The sight caught Josie completely off guard. Her heart filled like a helium balloon. She loved this man. The thought rattled her. Surely she hadn't admitted it last night to him, had she? She gripped the door frame, remembering the kiss.

What *had* followed it?

Her body suggested something had definitely happened. Was still happening. Just the sight of him seemed to caress her already-sensitive bare skin. Her nipples hardened to points against the fabric of the robe and a heat filled her, making her ache.

"I didn't know you knew how to change a diaper," she said, leaning against the doorjamb and trying to act as nonchalant as possible.

Clay looked up in surprise and grinned. "You should have seen me last night. It took a few tries to figure it out, and I still haven't got it down yet."

His gaze lit on hers, sending a shock of desire through her.

She walked over to the dressing table and Ivy. Clay had managed to get one side of the diaper attached. The other flapped in the breeze Ivy was making with her legs and arms. "About last night—"

"No need to apologize," he said, resuming his diaper changing.

Apologize? What did she have to not apologize for?

Ivy kicked and giggled and tried to get up, but he finally got the other half of the diaper ends together. He swooped the toddler up and into Josie's arms, smiling at the two of them as if they made a picture he couldn't resist.

Ivy wrapped her arms around Josie's neck, but her attention was on Clay. She seemed fascinated by him. Ivy hadn't been around many male role models. Not that Josie had ever thought of Clay as a role model for her daughter. Until now. The realization did more than surprise her.

"About last night—" she began again.

"I've been thinking a lot about Odell," Clay said, as if he thought that's what she meant.

Not hardly. Last night's horror had been blurred by waking up this morning, all warm and fuzzy, along with her body's continued reaction to Clay since she'd gotten up.

"I called a judge in Texas to get permission to open Odell's grave, and I had his dental records picked up." Clay obviously had pull in high places. "With a little luck, we'll know by this afternoon—"

"Did we make love last night?" she interrupted.

He looked up in surprise, his eyes widening. A lazy smile played at his lips. "You don't remember?"

"No, I don't," she admitted.

"I'd like to think that if we'd made love you'd remember," he said, sounding as if he was only half joking.

She met his gaze, her tongue stuck to the roof of her mouth for a moment. She licked at her lips but had the good sense not to say anything.

"Ivy interrupted us," he finally said. "I went to check on her. By the time I got back, you were sound asleep."

She nodded, feeling as if there had to be more. Or maybe her body had just ached for more. "I thought I remembered you in bed with me," she said as she put Ivy down, then tugged the robe tighter around her.

His smile broadened; his dark eyes bored into hers as if her words and her movements amused him. "I couldn't find a blanket, almost froze to death on the couch. I had no idea Montana was so cold in May." The heat of his gaze sent a lightning bolt through her. "I finally crawled in bed with you and got warm."

At least she wasn't losing her mind. Not entirely.

"But nothing happened." He seemed to wait to see how she felt about that.

"It's probably for the best," she said as she turned toward the kitchen and away from him, not wanting him to see the disappointment in her expression. "Hungry? I think I have some elk sausage Ruth's brother made."

Starved, Clay thought. But not for elk sausage. Or breakfast. He watched Josie walk down the stairs to the kitchen, pretty sure she had nothing on under the robe. The memory of her naked body pressed against his filled him with a yearning desire to take her back to bed. But that wasn't going to happen, he realized as Ivy came toddling to him.

"Panquakes," she said, gazing up at him with those big brown eyes and that cherub face. "Panquakes?"

Josie called back, "She wants to know—"

"If I like pancakes," he said, sweeping the baby up into his arms as he trailed her mother down to the kitchen.

"I love pancakes," he said, surprising himself by giving Ivy a kiss on her fat little cheek. His gaze lifted to Josie. She seemed a little surprised as well, as if she wasn't sure she knew him. He hardly recognized himself.

He'd come here to catch a thief and recover the jewels. He'd expected to catch Josie in that same net. What had changed his mind about her?

Or had he changed his mind? He studied her for a moment. Did he really believe she was innocent? He damned sure wanted to. Or maybe he just wanted her so badly that it didn't matter.

Either way, it wasn't like him. Not By-the-Book Jackson. He'd changed. Seeing her with Ivy, seeing her with the horses, seeing a woman he hadn't known in Texas. Maybe he just hadn't let himself get to know her.

He smiled to himself, remembering last night. He wanted to get to know her better. She was definitely some kind of rare woman and he wanted her. More than he could have ever imagined he could want a woman again.

Was it possible she wanted him as much as he did her? He thought about her reaction last night and again this morning in broad daylight. The image of her hard nipples pressed against the thin robe made him groan inwardly.

"I make a mean pancake," he said, desperately trying to get his mind on something else besides her lush body.

"You cook?" she asked in surprise.

He grinned, his gaze dropping from her eyes to her lips.

She ran her tongue over her lower lip, then caught her lip between her teeth. When he met her eyes again, he saw the warning. Please don't do this. Not now. But soon.

"Pancakes," he said, heading for the fridge. "All I need is flour, eggs, milk and a little baking powder."

"Panquakes!" Ivy shrieked.

"I think Ivy better help me," he said, lifting her up onto the counter beside him.

Josie groaned. "You don't know what you're letting yourself in for."

"Got an apron?" he asked.

She pulled one out and held it up. "Ruth made this one for me." It had embroidered flowers and lots of ruffles on it. She arched one fine brow, daring him to wear it.

He'd never been one to back down from a dare, and this morning he'd have done anything to see Josie smile. He took the apron and put it on, making her laugh. He liked to make her laugh. And Ivy, too.

"Want to learn how to break an egg?" he asked the toddler as Josie set about cooking the sausage.

Thirty minutes later, the kitchen looked as though a northerner had blown through. Flour dusted the counter, floor, him and Ivy. Egg ran down the front of the cabinet and batter ringed the bowl in splattered drying drops.

But he and Ivy had fried up a batch of perfectly browned pancakes to go with the elk sausage Josie had cooked.

"Don't worry," he said at Josie's disapproving look at the mess he and Ivy had made. "I also do my own dishes."

She eyed him askance. "What have you done with the real Clay Jackson?"

"Maybe you just never knew him," he suggested seriously.

"Maybe not," she agreed, her gaze holding his for a long electric-filled moment.

They sat down to breakfast, pulling the high chair up between them. Clay watched Josie take her first bite of his pancakes. Her eyes widened in surprise. She looked over at him.

"These are really good," she exclaimed.

He just grinned, having a hard time keeping his eyes—let alone his hands—off her. He couldn't wait to kiss her again. He couldn't wait to get her back into that bed. It was hard to concentrate on anything with her sitting there, naked under the robe, her blond hair bed-mussed, sleep still lingering in her eyes.

The elk sausage was spicy and a perfect complement to the pancakes, as was Ruth's huckleberry syrup.

They ate in a relaxed, companionable silence. It seemed so right, sitting here with Josie and Ivy, eating breakfast, that he hated it when his cell phone rang just as they'd finished.

Judge Branson? Clay answered the call, his body feeling numb and weak. "Clay Jackson."

"You said to get back to you as quickly as possible," the judge said, all no-nonsense. "Had that body exhumed. Sent off samples for DNA testing with a rush request. But I have to tell you, I think it's a waste of good money to run the DNA. Odell Burton's dental records matched the body's."

"What about the ring?"

"No jewelry was buried with the body. Family says they had a break-in a few months ago. Bunch of stuff was stolen, including Odell's ring. By the way, you remember O.T. Burton, Odell's father? Well O.T. says he doesn't want to hear Odell's name again and that this had better be the end of it. Anything else?"

"No, thanks, Judge."

He hung up and stood for a moment without

turning around. He could feel Josie nearby and hear Ivy chattering up a storm as if telling her mother a story. He closed his eyes tightly for a moment, in silent thanks.

"Odell's dead," he said quietly as he turned to face her.

"They're sure?"

He nodded. "No mistake. The dental records matched. The judge sent off DNA samples as well, but it's definite. Odell's dead. As for his ring, O.T. says it was stolen along with some other stuff a couple of months ago."

She sank down onto the couch, her body shaking with relieved sobs as she pulled Ivy into her arms. He watched her hug her daughter, washed with an ocean of emotions.

The sound of a vehicle coming up the hill drew his attention to the window. A sheriff's car pulled up beside his pickup and parked.

"Looks like we have company," he said to Josie as the sheriff climbed out and started toward the cabin.

Chapter Ten

It definitely *looked* like a map. But Josie didn't recognize any of the pencil markings on the sheet of the once tightly folded paper. Not that there were many markings. Five *X*'s along a line that wound around in a U-shape, almost a circle.

"Have any idea what it might be?" the sheriff asked. He'd taken a seat at the quickly cleared kitchen table, a file folder in front of him from which he'd pulled out a copy of the map he'd found on Raymond's body. "Or if it might have any relevance to Degas's death?"

She stared at the sheet of paper, fear filling her, but nothing on the map looked in the least bit familiar. It looked as if a child had drawn it. Crude. Simple. Frightening in the way the words had been printed. Something in the slant of the handwriting that sent a shaft of horror through her.

The only words on the map were Start by one

open end of the line, followed by Pit as the line continued down and around, then Garden, Waterfall, End, Paradise and Finish.

The word End had been circled in red ink.

She shivered, hugging herself as she looked up at the sheriff, and shook her head.

"How about you?" he asked Clay.

Clay shrugged and shook his head.

The sheriff leaned back in his chair and studied Clay for a long moment. "Raymond was wanted in Texas for questioning in a robbery two years ago."

Clay said nothing.

"I understand that the thieves were never caught and the cache of jewels never recovered," he continued, eyeing Clay. "I also know that you used to be in law enforcement and that you still do some consulting work. But you realize you have no authority to investigate a crime in the state of Montana."

"Like I said, I'm on vacation," Clay said with a shrug. "I didn't even know Josie was in the state." His gaze shifted to her. "It's a smaller world than I ever imagined."

The sheriff glanced over at her. He didn't look convinced but didn't press it. He picked up the copy of the map and slipped it back into a file marked Degas.

"We also found a stolen cell phone in Degas's

car.'' He seemed to hesitate before sliding another piece of paper across the table toward them. ''From what we can gather, Raymond Degas made three calls from the phone.''

She could feel Clay's gaze on her, hard and questioning. Was he thinking that Raymond might have called her? That her number at the ranch would be on the list? Oh, no, could Raymond *have* called her?

Her chest constricted as she looked down at the three numbers printed on the sheet. Relief swept over her. All three phone numbers had Texas area codes.

Then she recognized one of the numbers on the list and her heart stopped.

Clay studied the list as well, but his relief to see that Josie's number wasn't on the sheet of paper was short-lived. He stared down at the phone numbers. He knew all three.

A wave of confusion hit him as his gaze flicked up to Josie's. She'd paled, her eyes wide with shock.

''You recognize any of the numbers?'' the sheriff asked.

Clay could feel the sheriff's intent gaze. Lying wouldn't do any good.

''Yes,'' he said, looking away from Josie and the fear he saw. ''They're to the San Antonio area. The first number is the O'Malley Ranch.''

The sheriff looked at Josie. Clay saw that the cop already knew who the calls had been made to. He just wanted to know why. So did Clay.

"Any reason Raymond Degas would call your family?" he asked her.

Josie shook her head.

Clay offered an explanation. "To let them know he'd seen Josie and that she was all right?"

The cop's gaze shifted back to Josie. "Your family didn't know where you were?"

"Look, sheriff—"

"Let the lady answer," the sheriff interrupted him.

Josie seemed to have regained her composure. "To put it simply, I found myself pregnant. Where I come from that calls for a shotgun wedding. I didn't want to marry the baby's father. So I left. I haven't kept in touch with my family."

"Well, they know now," he said disapprovingly, then he looked at Clay again, waiting.

"The other numbers are to O.T. Burton and the Williams Gallery," Clay said, having done horse business with O.T. and consulting with Williams. "I have no idea why Raymond would call either of them."

The sheriff's smile never reached his eyes. "Funny, but that's what both parties said when I talked to them. I understand Degas ran with one of the Burton boys—Odell? And that both were suspects in the jewel robbery, but Odell is dead. He was killed in a car crash not long after the robbery.''

Clay could feel Josie tense in the chair next to him.

''And Brandon Williams, the owner of the gallery, is a collector. It was his jewels that were stolen.'' The sheriff's gaze locked onto Clay's. ''He seems to think you're up here looking for his jewels and the crooks.''

Clay didn't bat an eyelash. Didn't speak. Just waited, knowing the cop knew exactly what was going on here. But there wasn't anything he could do about it without proof.

''Do you have any leads on Raymond's death?'' Josie asked into the brittle silence.

The sheriff held Clay's gaze for a few seconds longer, then dropped it to the sheet of phone numbers. He slipped the paper back into the file and stood up to leave. ''It's still under investigation,'' he said without looking up. ''I may need to talk to you both again.'' He gave them both a warning look. ''Don't leave town.''

CLAY STOOD AT THE WINDOW and watched the sheriff drive away, wondering about the scared look he'd seen in Josie's eyes when she'd seen the map and the phone numbers.

What was it she was so afraid of? Not Odell

Burton. He was dead. Then what? Damn the woman. What was she hiding?

He turned at the sound of her footfalls behind him, his head spinning. Maybe Raymond had called the O'Malleys to tell them he knew where Josie was. Maybe. It just didn't feel right. Why would Raymond do that? Unless money was involved. Clay just couldn't see Shawn O'Malley paying someone like Raymond, even for that kind of information.

But what bothered him most was why Raymond called the other two numbers. Odell's father, O.T. Burton, had never had any use for Raymond. Nor much use for Odell, from the sound of it.

But it was the third number, the call to Williams Gallery, that shook him the most.

He'd dialed Brandon Williams's number the moment the sheriff had left. No answer. He didn't leave a message. This was something he wanted to discuss person to person.

As he watched Josie come into the room with Ivy he noticed her worrying her lower lip with her teeth. Was she upset about the calls Raymond had made or the map?

"So you didn't recognize the map the sheriff found on Raymond?" he asked.

Her gaze jerked up to his and he kicked himself for sounding so suspicious. But damned if he wasn't. Damned if he wasn't getting more suspicious as the days went on.

"I told the sheriff the truth, Jackson. I have no idea what it was. It just—" She let out a sigh and put Ivy down with her toys before heading for the kitchen.

"It just what?" he asked, following her. "Sit down and talk to me. I'm cleaning this up."

Surprisingly, she didn't argue. She sat, kneading her hands nervously in front of her on the table.

"It just gave me a bad feeling, that's all," she said, and put her hands in her lap. "It scared me, but I don't know why."

She fell silent as he began to wash the dishes. "Let me dry, please. I need something to do."

He nodded, studying her as she pulled a clean dish towel from the drawer. Ivy joined them to play in the toy drawer.

"Why would Raymond call Burton," she asked after a moment.

He shook his head, wondering if Raymond had some reason to think Odell was alive—just as Josie had. Maybe Raymond really believed that Odell had been the one who'd shot him. Hadn't Josie thought she heard him say "Odell did it"? Did someone want them to believe that Odell was alive? But why? And who would do that?

"Who identified Odell's body after the crash?" she asked out of the blue.

"O.T. The identification was based on the watch and ring. The body was too burned for anything else."

"Then dental records weren't checked?" she asked.

He shook his head. "It hadn't seemed necessary at the time. But Judge Branson said the records matched."

She nodded and began to stack the clean plates in the cupboard.

He finished cleaning the kitchen with Josie's help. A dense silence seemed to fall over the cabin as they finished.

"There's something I need to do. Would you watch Ivy for me?"

SHE CALLED FROM OUT on the porch, dialing the familiar number, her fingers trembling.

It rang once, then another two times. No one was home.

Someone picked up. "Hello."

Just the sound of her father's voice choked her up. Tears welled in her eyes and her voice broke. "Dad?"

"Josie." It sounded like a prayer. "Oh, Josie, thank God you called."

She couldn't speak.

"Are you all right?"

It wasn't what she'd expected him to say. She

thought he'd be angry and upset about her leaving, about her not calling before, about Ivy.

"Yes," she managed to answer, all her homesickness for Texas and her family flooding her with tears. "I've missed you."

"Me, too, baby."

They talked for a long time. She told him about Ivy and her horse training. He told her about the ranch and Texas and her brothers. Then her father grew quiet.

"Josie," he said after a moment. "When your mother died and left me a little girl to raise, I was scared to death. What did I know about little girls? I thought if I was tough on you like I was with the boys…" His voice trailed off. "I'm sorry I wasn't there for you."

"You did fine, Dad. This was something I had to do on my own."

"It sounds like you've done all right."

She wanted to correct him and tell him she'd messed up. Big time. But she hoped that she could right her mistakes before she saw her father—just as she'd sworn on her great-grandmother's memory she would do.

"You know Raymond Degas called here," her father said. "He had some fool notion that Odell was still alive."

Her heart thudded in her chest. "I know. But he was wrong."

"That's good." He seemed to hesitate. "When the sheriff called, he said someone killed Raymond. They find his killer?"

"Not yet."

Silence.

"Are you considering coming home, Josie?"

She desperately wanted to. Wanted her father and brothers to see Ivy. And Ivy to have her family around her. "I want to."

"Good, I was hoping you'd say that." He sounded relieved.

"I just need to finish what I started up here, Dad."

"I love you, Josie. Be careful."

"I love you, too, Dad."

She hung up and let all the pent-up emotions flow, then she dried her eyes and went inside.

HE STUDIED HER as she entered the living room. She'd pulled on a sweater, jeans and boots when the sheriff stopped by. Clay missed the robe and the way the thin fabric hugged her curves.

"How did it go?" he asked, suspecting she'd called home.

She nodded and smiled through fresh tears. "Dad wants me to come home."

Even a man as stubborn and hard-nosed as Shawn O'Malley had some sense, it seemed.

He wondered about his own good sense. Or if

he had any when it came to Josie. He'd made so many mistakes. Last night she'd been in a confessing mood. She'd wanted to tell him something, had seemed desperate to unburden herself.

But he'd stopped her. He'd been afraid of what she was going to say. He knew he'd have to hear it eventually. One way or the other. But not last night.

"Where's Ivy?" she asked.

He'd played with her until she couldn't keep her eyes open. "I put her down for her nap."

"Thank you."

"No problem. I enjoy her."

He thought he saw pain behind her tears. Why did he fear he'd made more mistakes with her than even he knew about? Or worse, that he was about to make another one?

"We need to talk," he said.

She nodded and brushed at the tears.

He reached out to cup her cheek in the palm of his hand, his thumb brushing across her lips, her soft, smooth cheek. "But first, I want to make love with you."

Her gaze never wavered. What he saw in her eyes almost leveled him. She kissed the pad of his thumb, her eyes filled with a need that mirrored his own.

He swept Josie up into his arms and carried her up the stairs to the bedroom, across from Ivy's, all reason and logic and suspicion discarded as quickly as he planned to discard their clothing. He wanted her. And he planned to have her. Right now. Later he'd deal with whatever she had to tell him, he told himself, as he closed the door.

She opened to his kiss, offering her mouth, encouraging him to explore deeper, as if he would find her every secret in the dark recesses. She clung to him, moaning softly as she kissed him back with a matching intensity that aroused and excited him.

This was nothing like the images that had haunted him. Nothing like the slow, sensual way she'd come to him that night in Texas in the dream. This was wild and hot and hurried. Filled with aching need. A fire that could only be put out with more fire.

She unsnapped his western shirt, jerking it open, flattening her palms to his bare skin as if she needed to feel him as desperately as he did her.

He released her lips only long enough to pull the light cotton-knit sweater over her head. His fingers unhooked the no-nonsense bra she wore, releasing her breasts to his waiting hands. He cupped them, thumbing the already-hard nipples, his desire heightening at just the sight of her.

She groaned and reached for his belt buckle. "Please, Clay."

They joined, coupled in a frantic need for release. He filled her and she fulfilled him in a dance as old as life.

When the release came, he felt as if a dam had broken. Not just for him, but for Josie, too, as if this had been the first time in a long time for her as well. A very long time.

They lay holding on to each other as if in a windstorm. But the real storm had passed, hadn't it?

He pushed himself up just enough to look down into her eyes. The last thing he wanted to do was break the connection between their bodies. He had hoped that having her would finally put an end to the years of yearning. But as he looked down at her, he knew he would never be free of her spell. He would want her again and again. He already did.

Her wide blue eyes stared up at him with a look of surprise and wonder and sated peace. Her blond hair curled wetly around her face. Her arms still locked around him as if she didn't want their bodies to separate any more than he did.

He stared into her eyes. A trickle of sweat rolled down his chest to pool in the hollow of her belly button. The breeze from the open window drifted over him, chilling his exposed flesh.

As he looked down at her, one clear thought

lodged itself in his brain like a splinter that refused to come out.

"We've done this before," he said, his voice deadly quiet and just as deadly sure.

Chapter Eleven

Josie stared into his eyes. "You aren't serious?"

He seemed dumbfounded, stunned. He *was* serious.

"You *really* don't remember," she said, staring up at him, as shocked as he looked.

Josie felt her heart lurch. She searched his gaze, wishing for the need, the desire, the fulfillment, the peace she'd seen just moments before. But all the warmth had gone out of his dark eyes. They stared down at her, hard, cold and accusing.

Her throat closed, her mouth dry as dust. He hadn't moved. Their bodies were still united. Slowly, she unlocked her arms from his back, but still he didn't move to let her up.

"Tell me," he whispered.

"Yes, we did this before."

She felt cold suddenly. From his gaze. From the breeze. She could feel him pulling away from her, although he still hadn't moved.

"When?"

"The night by the creek."

"Which night?" His gaze locked with hers.

All these months she'd thought he'd regretted their lovemaking—and he hadn't even *remembered* it! How could that be? The fall he'd taken from Diablo? Or the booze he'd consumed? Or had he not wanted to remember it, just as she'd originally thought?

"You got into a fight with Odell," she said, watching his face, "and took off on Diablo. You'd been drinking."

He pulled away, leaving an emptiness inside her, heart-deep. The cool breeze rushed over her bare, sweaty skin, chilling her.

Hurriedly she struggled to get into her clothing, needing something between her and the unbearable look in his eyes. Out of the corner of her eye, she watched him dress, his fingers working methodically while hers fumbled clumsily.

"You really don't remember," she said to his rigid back.

"No."

He sounded as cold as she felt. He didn't remember and now he thought she'd lied to him. Kept it a secret. If their lovemaking had been the only secret she'd kept these past two years, maybe then he could understand why she'd done what she had. Maybe then he could forgive her.

But as she finished dressing, pulling on her boots, she looked over at him. He sat on the end of the bed, his face set in granite. He jerked on his boots, the muscles in his arms bulging with the effort. Then he sat, staring straight ahead, his hands gripping the edge of the bed, his jaw set.

No, she thought, understanding and forgiveness were the last two things she could expect from Clay Jackson.

He fought to rein in the rush of emotions. Betrayal. Shock. Hurt. Anger. All bombarding him at once. Blurring his thoughts. Making him sick.

He stared at the wall, gripping the mattress as if it was all that was holding him together, unable to look at her. Unable to corral his thoughts any more than he could the turmoil of emotions.

Realization came slowly, awkwardly. It hadn't been a dream.

He loosened his grip on the bed as he looked over at her. Memories of the night by the creek flashed as bright as falling stars.

"You rode Diablo."

She nodded. "I'd been working with him, trying some of the techniques I'd seen other trainers use, techniques I'd read about."

And those techniques had worked. He remembered the way she'd ridden. No wonder he hadn't been able to believe it. She'd been able to ride a horse he had fought, a horse that had finally defeated him.

"Why didn't you say something the next day?"

Her brow shot up. "I just assumed you preferred to forget it as if it never happened."

The memory of that night had haunted him for two years. But he *hadn't* believed it had happened for so many reasons. Why was that?

He stared at her. Because he'd refused to believe she could ride Diablo. Refused to believe she could ride that well. His lack of faith in her shocked him.

But he knew it had been more than that. If he'd admitted to himself what had happened between them that night, he'd have had to admit how he felt about her.

He raked a hand through his hair, sick inside. He looked at her, her face still flushed from their lovemaking, it all coming back. Everything.

"Why did you come to me that night?" he asked, his voice sounding as tortured as he felt.

She looked away, but not before he'd seen the pain in her eyes. "Surely you know that I've always wanted it to happen." She shifted her gaze back to him. "When Diablo came back without you, I figured you'd been thrown. Without thinking, I got on the horse and rode out to find you."

"And you found me."

She nodded. "You looked so desolate, so hurt, I—"

"You felt sorry for me," he said in disgust.

Her eyes filled with tears and a mixture of emotions that pulled at his heart as she shook her head. "I wanted you," she whispered.

The honesty in her words stunned him. He wanted desperately to reach for her, to take her in his arms, to make up for all the hurt and pain they'd both suffered.

But a memory tugged at him, a feeling of dread at its heels. "That night by the creek, you were a…"

"A virgin?" Her gaze narrowed; tiny sparks flashed in the blue of her eyes. "That was another reason you didn't believe it happened, wasn't it? You refused to believe you might be wrong about me. That I might not be as wild as you were determined I was."

Her accusation hit its mark. Bull's-eye. He *had* believed the worst of her, but he realized now it had been less from her spirited antics and more to do with his own hurt. He'd *wanted* to believe the worst about her. Because he'd felt vulnerable around her. He'd known instinctively she was the one woman who could get to him.

He stared at her proud profile. "It wasn't you. It was me. I was…" The words didn't come easily. "I was scared. After Maria— I didn't want to get involved."

"I know." She turned slowly to look at him, but instead of anger in her gaze, he saw deep sadness.

His chest constricted, his throat went dry. He swallowed, afraid to ask the one question he now desperately needed answered. "Did you and Odell ever—"

"No," she said, anticipating his question. "I never had sex with Odell. I've never made love with anyone…but you."

The realization slammed him back, knocking the wind from him. He gripped the bed again and held on. It took him a moment to finally form the words. "Ivy is my daughter," he said, hearing the truth as he said them.

"Yes."

JOSIE WANTED TO RECOIL from the horrible pain that twisted his handsome face into a mask of despair. He threw back his head and let out a cry that froze her blood. A cry of pure anguish.

She reached for him, needing to comfort him. But he moved away from her before she could touch him.

He backed up against the bedroom wall, his hands out in front of him as if to shield him from her words. "You let me think she was Odell's."

"You're the one who saw Odell in her."

He nodded, his eyes dark and moist. "What was

I to think? I didn't remember that we'd made love.''

''Didn't you? Didn't you remember any of it?'' She saw the answer in his face.

He slammed a fist against the wall with a curse. ''Why, dammit? Why didn't you tell me when you realized you were pregnant?''

She didn't want to get into all the reasons. Not now. ''Because I believed it wouldn't have been the best thing for me or my child.''

''*Our* child, damn you. Ivy is *our* child! I had a right to know. I had a right to decide what was the best for our child.''

Her heart pounded. ''What would you have done if I'd told you?''

''I would have—'' He looked around as if the answer were in this room. He closed his eyes.

''I knew you wouldn't have believed Ivy was yours.'' Why did he believe it now?

He lifted his head slowly, sadness softening his handsome face. ''But once I knew she was mine, I would have married you.''

''You would have forced me to marry you whether it was what I wanted or not,'' she said angrily. The last thing she'd wanted was a loveless marriage. ''I did what I thought was best for Ivy and me.''

The phone rang, making her jump. She reached for it before it could ring a second time. ''Yes?'' She listened for a few moments. ''Yes, thank you for calling.'' She hung up and looked at Clay, tears in her eyes. ''That was the sheriff. They have a suspect in custody. A man who was seen drinking with Raymond at the Toston bar. They found the murder weapon in the man's car.'' Odell didn't kill Raymond. Because he was dead. ''It's over.''

''If you think that, Josie, you're dead wrong.''

HE HEARD IVY COMING AWAKE in the room across the hall. Ivy. His daughter.

Josie wiped her eyes and looked up at him. Neither spoke for a few moments. Ivy let out another cry.

Josie slid off the bed and headed across the hall.

He stood for a few moments, too shaken to move. He could still smell her on his skin. The same way their lovemaking had been branded in his mind. His anger seemed to overwhelm him.

He trailed after Josie, stopping in the doorway to watch her with Ivy. His daughter. Some of his anger dissipated at the sight of her. He tried to tell himself that Josie had done what she thought was right for her baby. Their baby.

But he couldn't. She should have told him. He had a right to know. Ivy was his, too.

He knew he needed time to think. But for the life of him, he had no idea where they went from here. It scared him. Now that he knew Ivy was his, it changed everything. Surely Josie realized that.

He watched her change the toddler, then put her down on the floor. Ivy scrambled over to him, holding out a worn teddy bear in her hand.

He looked into her large, lash-fringed brown eyes and felt a jolt, heart-deep. "Ivy," he whispered as he reached down to pick her up. He could smell her sweet baby scent as he wrapped his arms around her. Tears burned his eyes.

Over Ivy's small shoulder, he met Josie's gaze. But he refused to let her tears touch the wall of ice he'd built around his heart toward her.

He closed his eyes and hugged his daughter to him, awed and humbled and scared.

"She'll be hungry after her nap," Josie said.

He nodded, realizing how little he knew about his daughter. His gut constricted with regret at all he'd lost. Would he ever be able to forgive Josie? Forgive himself?

He followed her downstairs, carrying his daughter, Ivy's face against his, her arms around his neck.

The pull had always been there. He'd felt something for this child the moment he'd laid eyes on her. Had he known but just refused to admit the truth?

JOSIE COULDN'T BEAR to look at him. She busied herself making a peanut butter and jelly sandwich for Ivy.

When she turned, she saw he still held his daughter, his face filled with anguish. She watched him press a kiss to Ivy's cheek, then put her down. The expression on his face as he looked at his daughter broke her heart.

He didn't look at her as he turned and strode from the room, the screen door slamming behind him.

She closed her eyes, willing back the tears, but her heart filled with images of Clay and Ivy. Their laughter mingling. Their dark eyes accusing her.

What had she done?

Two years ago, she'd believed Clay would make a terrible father and an even worse husband. She'd believed he'd regretted their lovemaking and wanted nothing to do with her. Yes, he'd been wrong about her, had purposely thought the worst of her to protect himself from his feelings.

But what she'd done to him was so much worse. She'd kept him from his daughter. She'd underestimated the man she loved.

"I'm sorry, Clay," she whispered after him.

Ivy chattered up a storm as Josie put her into the high chair and fed her. "Everything's going to be all right now." She repeated the words, praying somehow they would come true.

Someone knocked at the front door. Clay. He'd come back. She pulled a peanut-butter-and-jelly-faced Ivy from her high chair and hurried to the door.

But it was Mildred peering through the screen door.

"Are you all right?" Mildred asked.

Josie smiled, but the tears gave her away.

"What did he do now?" Mildred said, going to the kitchen, straight to the coffeepot.

"It isn't what you think," Josie said, following behind her. Ivy wriggled to be put down, but not before Josie cleaned up her face and hands. Ivy hurried to her cupboard to pull out all of the toys.

"You told him, didn't you?" Mildred said, her hands on her hips as the coffee began to fill the pot. "You told him he is Ivy's father."

Her mouth gaped open.

"Oh, Josie, Ruth and I both knew the moment we laid eyes on him."

She stumbled over to a chair and plunked down. It had been a long day. Too much had happened. She rubbed her temples, wondering what Mildred would say if she knew that she'd just made love with him again this afternoon. "I had to tell him."

"Of course you did," Mildred agreed. "I'm sure you had your reasons for not telling him before. What happens now?"

She shook her head. "Oh, Mildred, it's all so complicated."

"Love usually is."

Her gaze froze on the woman. "Love? What makes you think—"

"Oh, please. I'm not *that* old that I don't know love when I see it."

Josie leaned her elbows on the table and dropped her chin into her hands. "Clay and I have always been like oil and water. He's never understood me any better than I did him. Now too much has happened. We'll never be able to get past it. We're all wrong for each other. We always have been and nothing can change that."

"It already has," Mildred said, smiling. "Ivy. Ivy is the best of the two of you. She's proof that with love even two people like you and Clay can find some common ground."

Common ground. Josie thought of their lovemaking. Oh, they'd already found their common ground, all right. A sexual chemistry. But unfortunately that was shaky ground and nothing to build any sort of relationship on.

"Would you like me to stay?" Mildred asked.

Josie shook her head. "We'll be fine. The sheriff has a suspect in custody for Raymond Degas's murder." And Odell was dead. "We'll be just fine." She actually believed it. She got up to give Mildred a hug. "You go on home. I know you have things to do. But thanks for all your help. I really appreciate it."

"Charley asked me into town for dinner," Mildred said, grinning. "You think I should go?"

"Absolutely," Josie told her.

Mildred got a hug and a kiss from Ivy, then left. Josie watched her drive away, wondering where Clay had gone. He hadn't left for good. That much she knew.

The sun had dropped behind the mountains, leaving the day cool and a little dark. She made a light dinner for herself and Ivy, but opted to eat inside tonight because of the approaching storm. Thunder rumbled off in the distance.

She played with Ivy until the night turned black and the breeze coming through the window smelled of rain. She sensed static in the air she wasn't sure had anything to do with the storm. She couldn't quit thinking of Clay, the ache for him painful. Was he all right?

She bathed Ivy, dressed her in her favorite teddy bear pajamas and put her to bed just before the storm hit. Lightning lit the night outside her bedroom window. She tried to read, but finally gave up and turned out the light. The storm moved closer. Huge splintered bursts of lightning lit the sky, immediately followed by the cannon boom of thunder.

She pulled the blankets up to her chin, hoping the storm didn't wake Ivy and scare her. She wished Clay was here with them.

Finally, rain began to fall and the lightning and thunder moved on.

It was after three in the morning that Josie woke with a start, sitting upright in bed. At first she thought she'd heard something that had woken her. The rain had stopped. No sound came from inside or outside the cabin.

She turned on the lamp beside the bed, slid into her slippers and hurried to Ivy's room, suddenly afraid.

Ivy lay curled under her blanket sound asleep, her arms wrapped around her teddy bear.

Josie stood for a few minutes watching her, reassuring herself that her baby was fine. It must have just been a bad dream.

That's when she remembered what had dragged her from sleep. Raymond's last words. "Odell did it."

She'd thought he was trying to tell her who'd shot him. But he couldn't have meant that. Odell was dead. Then what had Raymond been trying so hard to tell her? Why would a dying man use his last breath if not to name his killer?

It felt like a light going off inside her head. A burst of knowledge, bright and blinding. *Not* "Odell did it." But "Odell *hid* it." The jewel collection.

That is what Raymond must have been looking for, just as Clay suspected. But if Odell hid it, wouldn't it be in Texas, unless—

She sensed movement from the open doorway. Whirling in that direction, she saw a large man in a western hat silhouetted in the doorway.

"Clay?"

But the moment she said his name, she knew it wasn't Clay.

A scream caught in her throat. No one would hear her but Ivy if she screamed. She spun around, frantically grabbing for a weapon in the dim light in the shadowy room. Her fingers closed over the base of a lamp as she heard him behind her.

He was on her before she could swing the lamp. His strong fingers clamped over her wrist and twisted hard. The lamp thumped to the floor.

Something hard smacked the side of her head. Stars splattered across her vision.

"Ivy!" It was her last thought before the darkness took her.

Chapter Twelve

Clay drove around for hours. Thinking. Remembering. Hurting. An unmerciful weight had settled on his chest, making merely breathing unbearable.

By the time he got back to Josie's cabin, he felt more excitement about being Ivy's father than anger toward Josie for keeping his daughter from him.

He understood why she'd done what she had. Understood the part he'd played. The confusion. The misunderstanding. And he blamed himself more than Josie.

But it didn't make it any easier.

He parked a little way from the cabin. No lights shone inside, not that he'd expected to see any. It was late. Josie and Ivy would be asleep.

He slid down in the front seat, pulled his Stetson down over his eyes and tried to sleep, craving some release from his thoughts. Worse, his feelings. Feelings of love so strong that he thought his heart would burst.

Ivy was his daughter.

And Josie? He didn't want to think about that right now. Couldn't.

Sleep came in fitful spurts, filled with haunting images, the interludes in between packed with waking panic.

His dreams were always the same. Josie riding up to his campfire on Diablo.

Only this time something was horribly wrong.

Just before daylight, he jerked awake, heart pounding, drenched in sweat, his mind suddenly clear. He *knew* how Josie had done it! He knew how she'd gotten the security plans to steal the jewels.

He flung open the pickup door and raced down the hill to the cabin, not caring about the hour, not caring about anything but confronting Josie. If he thought she'd dropped a bombshell on him yesterday, wait until today. And just when he thought it couldn't get any worse.

He pounded on the front door, waiting in the cool shadow of the porch. The moon sneaked toward the dark western horizon as if hoping to avoid the sun that now rimmed the mountain crest to the east. The early-morning darkness felt damp and cool and quiet.

He pounded again, needing desperately to break

that eerie silence, to make sense of what had happened two years ago.

Still no answer. She was probably expecting him and had no intention of answering the door. Or she'd taken off. But her truck was still parked in the yard.

He tried the door, surprised to find it unlocked. He frowned as he turned the knob and the door fell open and he stepped in.

He felt something under his boot soles. His heart took off at a gallop as he flipped on the living room light. On the floor were wood shavings from where the front door had been jimmied open.

His pulse pounded in his ears at a deafening tempo, his heart a thunder in his chest as he took the stairs two at a time.

A muted night-light gleamed from the empty bathroom. He swung to his left and into Josie's bedroom.

The light was on, the covers thrown back on the bed, the pillow balled near the edge, a hollow space still in the sheets where she'd been. But the bed was empty.

He swung around and raced across the hall into Ivy's room, flinging open the door, his gaze leaping to the crib. The first morning light bled in through the window. Even from the doorway he could see that the crib was empty.

A groan. His gaze swung to the dark corner of the room and the figure crumpled there.

He reached her in two strides, dropping beside her, his fingers going to her throat for a pulse, a prayer echoing in his head. "Please, God, please."

He felt a pulse. Strong. Strong like Josie.

She stirred, her eyelids flickering. Her lips moved but no sound came out.

Tears burned his eyes. He took a ragged breath. "Don't try to talk. I'm here. Everything is going to be all right," he whispered as he brushed the fine blond hair back from her face and felt the lump and the dried blood.

Her eyes jerked open. She blinked up at him, all that blue filled with confusion and pain. "Ivy." The word was only a whisper.

He felt his heart take off again. "Isn't she with Mildred?"

"No!" Josie tried to get up.

He held her down, a lump the size of Texas lodging in his throat as he looked over at the empty crib. "She was here?"

Josie nodded, tears coursing down her cheeks. "He took her."

"Who, Josie? Who took her?"

She began to cry, huge gut-wrenching sobs. "I didn't get a good look at him."

"It's all right."

"No, Clay," she said, trying to get up again. "I have to find Ivy."

He fought to breathe. "We'll find her, Josie. Just lie still for a moment, please."

The phone rang.

He stared down at her for an instant. "Stay here."

He charged into the bedroom, half-falling, half-sliding, and jerked up the phone. "Yes. Hello."

"It's Charley, Charley Brainard. Sorry to call at this hour, but I can't seem to find Mildred. It's just odd. All the lights are on, her car's here and her knitting is in the middle of the floor. I thought maybe something had happened over there, some reason she might have left in a hurry without her car?"

Clay felt the floor drop from under him. "No, we haven't seen her. But I'll let you know if I do."

He'd barely hung up the phone when it rang again.

A deadly silence filled the line, one he could barely hear over the frantic beat of his heart.

"Jackson." The voice was electronic, unrecognizable. "I have your daughter."

Clay could hear Ivy crying in the background and someone trying to soothe her. "If you hurt a hair on her head—"

"You are in no position to threaten me," the

voice snapped. "Listen carefully. I have Ivy and her baby-sitter."

Mildred?

"If you ever want to see Ivy again you will tell no one. No police. Don't underestimate me." Ivy's crying grew louder, and he realized that the voice on the other end of the line had moved closer to the toddler.

"Ivy. Let me talk to her." To his surprise the caller put the phone next to Ivy's mouth and ear. "Ivy?" The crying slowed. "Ivy. Ivy, honey." She stopped crying but still whimpered. He could see her in his mind's eye, her face red and tear-stained, her cupid's bow lips thrust out, eyes wide. His eyes. "Listen, sweetheart." His voice broke. "It's going to be all right. Can you hear me. It's…"

"Clay." He heard a sound behind him and turned to see Josie stumble into the room.

"Your mommy is here."

He handed the phone to Josie but stayed beside her so he could hear.

"Ivy? Ivy, darling."

He closed his eyes at the sound of Ivy's sweet voice. Then the electronic voice came back on.

"Jackson?"

He could hear Mildred in the background. She sounded scared but was trying to comfort Ivy.

"I'm here," he snapped, as angry as he was

afraid. "Who are you? What the hell do you want?" How do you know Ivy is my child?

"I want the jewels," the eerie, unreal voice said. "Josie has them."

Clay looked over at her. She *had* the jewels. Just as he'd suspected. And now someone had kidnapped their daughter for those damned rocks. He gritted his teeth, his gaze boring into her.

She shook her head, her eyes wild as she covered the phone. "I don't have the jewels," she whispered frantically. "You have to believe me, Clay. You of all people."

He stared at her, blinded by his anger, by his need to protect his child. Their child. Josie wouldn't lie about this, not with her daughter's life at stake.

The electronic voice was saying, "I'll call back with instructions for the trade tonight. If you—"

"Just a minute," he interrupted, "What makes you think Josie has the jewels?"

Silence. He feared the caller had hung up.

"The jewels had better still be in her great-grandmother's rodeo saddle where they were. And don't try to tell me that she doesn't have it. She'd never part with that saddle." Static. "Get the jewels and wait for my call. If you tell anyone, especially the police, you will never see your daughter again. Is that understood?"

Clay's gaze was still locked on Josie. His chest tightened. "Yes, I understand perfectly."

"One more thing." The electronically disguised voice set his nerves on edge. "You are to bring Josie O'Malley with you. No argument."

Clay felt a blade of pure ice sink into his heart. "Josie will be there."

"Do I have to remind you what will happen to the kid if you and Josie don't come alone?"

"No."

"Good. And don't forget the jewels or try to pull anything."

Who had taken Ivy? Someone who knew him. Knew Josie. Knew them both well. If he hadn't known better, he would have sworn that Odell Burton had come back from the grave.

"You'll get your jewels," he said through gritted teeth. "Just don't hurt my daughter. Or I'll kill you."

The line went dead.

"Oh God, Clay," she cried as she watched him hang up the phone. Her baby had been kidnapped. By some monster who thought she had the jewels in her great-grandmother's saddle?

She tried to hold back the hysteria, the irrational need to just sit and cry or scream and beat the wall with her fists. She had to keep her head. She had to help her baby.

Clay hadn't moved. He stood, his eyes closed,

his hands clenched into fists at his side, his face twisted in pain.

"Clay?" She reached for him, needing him to tell her that it was going to be all right, that they would get Ivy back, that he'd help her.

But when his eyes opened, she saw that it was much more than pain that burned in the darkness. Much more than anger.

"I know how Odell got the security plans," he said, his voice as hollow and strange as the man's on the phone.

Her heart stopped and it took all she could do to will it to keep beating. She'd lost everything. Clay would never believe her now. Not that he would have two years ago.

"It isn't what you're thinking."

He raised a brow. "You have no idea what I'm thinking."

"You think I betrayed you that night by the creek in Texas."

"Didn't you? Didn't you seduce me for my keys so you could get the security plans for Odell? That was the real reason you made love to me, why you came down to the creek, wasn't it? The damned jewels."

She opened her mouth but no words came out. Weakness seeped through her limbs. Not now. Don't let this be happening now. Her head ached.

But nothing like her heart. Ivy. Oh, Ivy. They had to find Ivy. They had to get her back.

She needed Clay to help her find their daughter. But he didn't trust her. He thought she'd seduced him for the security plans. That she'd endangered their child for the jewels. Or for Odell. Did he think she'd lied about that, too?

She looked at him, wanting to scream and cry and beat his chest to make him see that they had to trust each other. Now. For Ivy's sake.

Somehow she found the words. "I didn't know anything about Odell's plans to steal the jewels. That night when Diablo came back riderless, I rode Diablo because I was worried about you." She didn't tell him that she'd come to his ranch, looking for him. Dressed in a yellow sundress, feeling foolish and sexy and ready to do anything to get him to notice that she wasn't a kid anymore.

He said nothing. His gaze was unforgiving.

"I didn't just want you that night. I was in love with you. I had been for years."

He flinched, his gaze darker, harder. A muscle jumped in his jaw.

"When I crossed the creek, I saw you, sitting with your back against the trunk of that live oak. I saw something in your eyes. Or at least I believed I did. Heartache. And desire for me. I thought I recognized it because of my own."

- type=

She hoped he'd say something. But still he remained motionless, rigid with anger.

"I made love to you because I wanted you and I thought you wanted me, too. It was so incredible. I thought it had changed everything." She looked up and saw impatience in his gaze.

"I had fallen asleep in your arms," she continued, realizing that if he didn't believe this much, he sure as the devil wasn't going to believe the rest. "I woke near daylight to see Odell. He had something in his hand. I started to wake you, but he stopped me by holding up your keys, then slowly putting them back in our pile of clothing and leaving. I didn't know that he'd already taken the keys, made a copy of the security plans and was returning them when I caught him."

"He just happened to know I wouldn't be wearing my jeans that night beside the creek?" Clay said. "You expect me to believe that? How did he know where to find me?"

"He told me after the robbery that he'd followed you," she snapped, her nerves taut. "He'd planned to get the keys from you, one way or the other. My showing up just gave him a less confrontational way. This way he could hurt us both."

Tears welled in her eyes. She willed herself not to cry. She had to think of Ivy. Getting Ivy back. If Clay didn't believe her, then there was nothing she could do about that. There never had been.

He said nothing, but some of the anger seemed to dim in his gaze.

"It wasn't until after the robbery, before you caught Odell and me fighting outside my barn, that he told me what he'd done. How he'd implicated me in the robbery."

"Why would he do that?" Clay asked.

She looked at him and saw that he really didn't seem to understand the relationship the three of them had had.

"He wanted to hurt me, the way he felt I'd hurt him by making love with you," she said. "Unlike you, he knew I was a virgin and he knew why. He knew that you were the only one I wanted. He saw me losing my breakfast by the barn and guessed that I was pregnant with your baby. He knew you'd never believe me about the keys. He was determined that you wouldn't win." She let out a laugh that was so close to a sob her eyes filled with tears. "He thought you *wanted* to win me. He didn't know it had all been for nothing."

Clay looked away, battered by an onslaught of conflicting emotions. "So you ran?"

"I only thought of my baby. Our baby. I was determined to protect her. At all costs. I was afraid of what Odell would do. He swore he'd hurt her."

"But then Odell was killed," Clay pointed out. "You could have returned to Texas. You could have told me the truth."

"I didn't hear about Odell's death until a few months ago. I'd been planning to come back to Texas as soon as I had the money. I'd made a promise on my great-grandmother's memory that I would go back and try to make things right."

Clay didn't know what to think. She'd thought she loved him? His heart desperately wanted to believe she'd seduced him for any other reason than the jewels.

And that she hadn't told him the truth to protect Ivy.

If only he'd known about the baby. About Odell's threat. Maybe this wouldn't be happening now. What would Odell have done if Josie hadn't run? Would he have hurt her or her baby to keep Ivy from being born? Or would he have gotten the jewels out of the saddle, gotten caught, and this would have all been over?

"Let's get your great-grandmother's saddle," he said, not wanting to think let alone talk about that night right now.

But when he looked over at her, he saw her eyes widen. He felt a chill race over him. "Where is the saddle, Josie?"

"Oh, God, Clay. It's not here."

He felt his veins turn to ice. "What do you mean, it's not here? The kidnapper was sure you'd never part with it."

"No, I wouldn't. Under normal circumstances.

You asked how I was able to make it, pregnant and alone with no money. I pawned the saddle. It was the only thing I had of any value.''

He felt light-headed. The room seemed to spin. He pulled her to him, hanging on for dear life. ''You lost it!''

''No,'' she cried. ''I just can't get my hands on it quickly. The pawn shop is in Bozeman and I don't have enough money saved yet.''

He let go of her. ''Money is the least of our problems. I'll pay to get it back. Let's just hope the jewels are still inside.''

''How did they get there?'' she cried.

''I thought if anyone would know, it would be you,'' he said coldly. ''Get dressed. We can have a doctor check your head where you were hit. Then we'll be waiting at that pawnshop the moment it opens.''

SHE FELT AS IF SHE MIGHT fly into a million pieces. She hurriedly pulled on her clothes, her head aching, her heart pounding, fear making her weak and sick and crazy.

Clay drove them out of the ranch and headed toward Bozeman, thirty miles to the east. The sun shone blindingly bright in a cloudless blue sky. It should have been raining and dark and cold, the way it was in her heart.

But part of her held on to a small thread of hope.

Maybe Clay didn't believe her, but he was helping her. She'd never needed him more than she did now, but she could feel the wall between them. They'd never trusted each other. Nothing seemed to have changed. Except now Clay knew that Ivy was his daughter. And he blamed her because a kidnapper had her. Had taken her for some jewels she hadn't known were hidden in her great-grandmother's saddle.

"Clay, please talk to me. Say something."

"Let's just get the jewels. Then we can talk about what to do."

DUST COATED the pawnshop's windows, making it appear dark inside. Clay parked the truck on the side of the building. A bell tinkled over the door as they walked in. The place was a clutter of once-valued things that had been turned into ready cash. He just hoped the saddle was still here.

Josie pulled out her claim stub and handed it over the dirty counter to a tall, thin man with a bad complexion. He studied it for a moment.

"I want to pick up my saddle," she said nervously.

Clay could almost hear the thumping of her heart over his. Almost.

The man nodded and disappeared through a curtain into the back of the shop. Clay waited anxiously for him to return.

The clock on the wall ticked off the minutes.

The place was hot and smelled of too many people and their things.

When the man finally pushed through the curtain with the saddle under one arm, Clay could have kissed him.

Clay slapped a half-dozen bills down on the glass counter. "Will that cover it?"

The man looked up, studying Clay from under hooded eyes. "Got any identification?" he asked Josie.

She dug in her bag and showed him her Texas driver's license.

Slowly he picked up the money from the counter, counted it and put it into the till. Then he lifted the saddle, bypassing Clay to hand it to Josie.

She hugged it to her, tears welling in her eyes, and Clay followed her out the door.

"I should never have pawned it," she said as they walked to the truck.

He opened the door for her and hurried around to slide behind the wheel.

"You did what you had to do to survive. Your great-grandmother would have understood. She would have been proud of you, Josie."

He heard her crying softly as she held the saddle in her arms as if she held her daughter.

As he drove out of Bozeman, he watched his rearview mirror. But no one seemed to be following them. He could hear Josie working at the saddle.

''Are they in there?'' His voice broke.

A sob burst from her, then the tearful words, ''They're here. Oh, thank God, they're here.''

He let out a small sigh of relief. They had a long way to go. But at least now they had the damned jewels. And to think at one time, he thought once he found the jewels it would be over for good. How wrong he'd been.

JOSIE STARED AT THE PILE of sparkling jewels, hating them, hating Odell. ''I'm scared, Clay.''

He didn't say anything for a few moments. Then she looked over at him. His gaze shifted from the road to her. The cold, hard darkness she'd seen in his eyes was suddenly gone. He looked as scared as she did.

He loves Ivy, too.

With tears in his eyes, he pulled her over to him. She snuggled into him, desperately needing his warmth, his strength, desperately needing him. The father of her baby.

She closed her eyes and breathed in the scent of him, surrounded by his strong arms, protected. In his arms, she believed they would get Ivy back safely. In his arms, she believed they could conquer anything.

They reached the cabin with plenty of time to spare but hurried inside to wait for the call.

"The night Raymond died, I thought he'd whispered 'Odell did it.' But with Odell dead—" She looked over at him. "Raymond must have said 'Odell *hid* it.' The bag of jewels. I saw Odell coming out of my barn six weeks after the robbery. He said he'd been looking for me, but at the time, I thought he seemed…odd."

"That's probably when he put the jewels in the saddle."

"He just hadn't expected me to leave Texas like I did. He must have told Raymond where he'd hidden them before his death." She hesitated. "Clay, with both Raymond and Odell dead, then who has Ivy?"

Someone who knew where Odell had hidden the jewels. Someone who knew Clay. Knew her. Someone with a grudge against them.

He shook his head. "Someone Raymond or Odell told."

She nodded, but she could tell he was as scared as she was. The worst part was that they had no idea just who they were dealing with. Or what lengths he would go to. Why didn't the kidnapper call?

When the phone rang, they both jumped.

It took them both a minute of confusion to realize it was Clay's cell phone that was ringing.

"Jackson?" the voice demanded.

Clay shook his head at Josie to let her know it wasn't the kidnapper. "Judge Branson." His chest felt like someone had dropped a piano on it.

"We just got the DNA tests back. I'd put a rush on them for you." The judge let out a sigh. "The lab already had a sample of Odell's DNA from an earlier arrest. Jackson, that body in the grave—"

He knew. He'd known the moment he'd heard Judge Branson's voice on the other end of the line.

"We don't know who the hell it is, but it's not Odell Burton."

Chapter Thirteen

Josie saw it in Clay's body language. In the way he hung up the phone, his head bent, the weight of the conversation heavy on his broad shoulders.

When he looked over at her, she felt the floor drop out from under her. "Odell's alive."

Clay pulled her into his arms. "At least now we know who and what we're up against," he said, sounding almost relieved.

Her worst fears had come true. Odell Burton had her child. A child conceived by a man Odell hated and born to a woman he'd sworn to destroy.

"Oh, Clay, he'll kill her if he hasn't already."

"No, Josie," he said, pulling back to look into her face. He shook her gently, until her gaze locked with his. "He's just using Ivy to get to us. We have the advantage, though. We know Odell. And he doesn't realize that we're on to him."

She struggled to find hope in his words, in the

fierce, confident look in his eyes. "But Odell knows us, Clay. He'll anticipate anything we do."

"Josie, do you want to go to the police? It's your decision."

She stared at him in disbelief. "All these years of everyone telling me what to do and you pick *now* to let me make a decision like this?"

"I can make the decision, Josie, but you're Ivy's mother. It should be your decision."

She looked into his dark eyes. Ivy's eyes. "Knowing Odell, I'm afraid to do anything that might jeopardize our daughter's life. He's not bluffing. He'll kill Ivy if we call the police."

Clay let out a sigh. "I agree. Odell's too unstable for us to take any chances."

The phone rang again. This time they both knew who it would be.

JOSIE FELT NUMB as they drove out of Three Forks under a dark, hopeless night sky. The Jefferson River moved along dull as lead under the black rough edge of the mountains cut against the skyline.

She held the backpack with the bag of jewels in her lap, her fingers kneading the silken material, feeling the cold of the rocks beneath. Her emotions ran from hope to hate, from fear to murderous rage. She wanted to kill Odell. She thought she could have with her bare hands.

"We're going to have to work together," Clay said from beside her.

She nodded. She just wanted her daughter back. Whatever it took. But numb, frozen fear made her want to curl up in a ball and cry and pretend this wasn't happening.

Clay had repeated the kidnapper's instructions to her when he got off the phone. The words had again been electronically altered but now they knew why. Both she and Clay would have recognized Odell's voice.

They were to bring a backpack. It was to contain only two small flashlights, one votive candle, one pack of paper matches and the jewels. Nothing more.

At some point along the way, the backpack would be checked and they would be searched. If they brought anything else, especially any type of weapon, they would never know what happened to their child.

Clay drove southwest past Three Forks, taking Highway 287 toward Ennis. At the junction, he stopped to look under a large stone next to the stop sign. More instructions. He was to take Highway 2 toward Whitehall.

But as he got back into the truck, he let out a curse. "He's leading us to Lewis and Clark Caverns."

Josie felt herself go weak. "I'd forgotten about

his fascination with caves.'' It explained the odd mixture of items they had been instructed to bring in the backpack. It explained—

''The map!'' they both said in unison.

''The map the sheriff found on Raymond,'' Clay said excitedly. ''It's the inside of the caverns.''

Josie sat up a little straighter, hope rushing through her.

''Do you think you can draw it?'' he asked as she snapped on the cab light to dig in the glove box as he drove. She found a pen and a Burger King napkin. ''Wasn't Pit the first name on the map?''

''Yes.'' She quickly drew what she remembered with Clay's help. ''Remember the word End circled in red?''

''Yeah. I would imagine that's where he plans to make the trade,'' Clay said. ''And the word, Paradise just before the word Finish.''

''He thinks he'll have the jewels,'' she said, not wanting to voice her real fear. That for Odell, paradise would only be if he'd gotten the jewels, destroyed her and Clay—and won.

Clay found more instructions just before the turnoff for Lewis and Clark Caverns, not that he hadn't already anticipated what they would say. ''Go up the mountain and into the caverns. Keep going. More instructions will be posted once inside.''

The narrow paved road curled up the mountain in tight switchbacks. The headlights cut a narrow swatch through the dense trees, the darkness close and low.

The road ended in a small paved parking lot. Several small buildings stood against the night sky. Two vehicles sat in the lot. A rental car and an old pickup truck with local plates.

Clay drove in and parked away from both of them. He killed the engine and the headlights. A faint light glowed near one of the buildings.

"Oh, God, Clay, someone else is here," she whispered.

He took the backpack from her, saying nothing as he opened his door and got out. She followed, hurrying to catch up to him. He had the backpack slung over his shoulder and one of the flashlights in his hand. The golden disk of light bobbed across the pavement in front of him as Clay neared the only other light on the mountain.

Just as she caught up to Clay, he stopped and turned to try to shield her from something on the ground. At first all she glimpsed was the source of the faint light she'd seen from the truck. A flashlight lay on the ground, the beam dim as if the batteries were running low.

Past it, she caught sight of a pair of boots connected to two jeans-clad legs sticking out from behind the building.

Clay knelt down, then straightened. "The security guard," he whispered. "He's dead."

She glanced at the poor man on the ground. Her heart hammered, her pulse thundering at her temple. Odell had already killed once tonight and he had Ivy.

Her limbs suddenly felt as though they were made of stone. She stared at the mountain ahead, too afraid to move. Tears burned in her eyes. She wanted to howl like the wounded animal she was.

She felt Clay's hand on her face. He cupped her jaw and pulled her into him. She buried her face in his chest, absorbing the warm feel of his jacket, the safe feel of his arms around her.

"We're going to get her back," he whispered. "I promise you, Josie. You just have to trust me."

She could feel the steady beat of his heart against her cheek, his arms around her, strong but gentle. Trust, that was something they'd never had. She looked up into his face beneath the wide brim of his Stetson. Steely determination shone in his eyes. But something more. His love for Ivy.

"Trust me?" he whispered.

She straightened and let out a ragged breath. "I trust you."

"We can do this, Josie," he whispered as he brushed a tear from her cheek.

She nodded, catching his large, warm hand and bringing it to her lips before letting him go.

He handed her the flashlight and motioned for her to lead the way up the path to the cavern entrance. She took a step, then another, each growing a little stronger. Instead of looking ahead, she watched only the few feet of path she could see in front of her. One step at a time. Don't think. Just walk.

She did, trying to hold back the horrible thoughts that bombarded her. Trying to keep from looking off the steep drop to her left as the path climbed the mountain. Or looking too far into the future.

She had to believe in Clay. Believe in herself. She wasn't still that scared young girl that Odell had bullied in Texas. But he didn't know that. He would expect her to cower, to beg, to cry. That's the way he liked her.

She lengthened her strides, breathing in the night air, feeling strength in her legs, in her heart. She could hear Clay behind her and thanked God he was here.

The smell hit her first. Dead, cold air, wrought with an age-old dampness.

She slowed. A gaping hole yawned in the side of the mountain. The once locked, barred door that had sealed it shut now hanging open. Ivy's favorite teddy bear hung from one of the bars.

Clay gently pulled the worn teddy bear down, drawing it to his face. It smelled like her. He breathed in the scent of her, then pulled Josie to him, holding them both for a long moment.

Then he handed the bear to Josie.

She was crying softly, but when he met her gaze, her eyes gleamed with determination. His heart ached as he watched her hug the bear to her as she would have Ivy.

He stared into the dark, ominous opening. Unlike what he'd told Josie, Odell had every advantage. All they had was their love for their daughter.

An owl screeched somewhere nearby, giving him a start. In the distance, a car engine droned on the highway below them. Nothing but silence came from within the cave.

Unlike Odell, he'd never liked caves and didn't like the idea of being trapped underground with a madman. Worse yet, the last thing he wanted to do was take Josie in with him. But he knew neither of them had any choice.

Odell was calling the shots. At least for the moment.

"Stay close," he whispered to Josie as he pulled the second flashlight from the pack. "And remember what I said." His gaze met hers for a moment, then he pointed the flashlight beam into the caverns and stepped through the rock arch, with Josie close behind.

Inside, their footfalls echoed off the walls of carved stone. Their flashlights did little to hold back the darkness. Clay moved slowly at first, feeling his way, expecting Odell to ambush them at any time.

They hadn't gone far when he felt Josie clutch at the back of his jacket, grabbing a handful of cloth. Overhead, the ceiling came alive.

She let out a small choked cry as dozens of bats took flight, a scurry of wings and dark movement just inches above their heads.

"You all right?" he whispered back to her.

The hand on his back released its hold.

The path dropped downward in a series of cramped rock steps. At one point, he thought he heard a baby crying. He stopped to listen but could hear nothing but the drip of water deeper in the caverns, deeper in the endless darkness.

Not far in, they passed a shaft that dropped down to an open room. The Pit on the map Raymond had on him when he was killed?

The narrow path wound down another set of tight, steep steps that opened into a room filled with stalactites and stalagmites, then down along a small tunnel.

This time when it opened up, he saw that they were now at the bottom of the pit. Clay stopped to look up, feeling the hair rise on the back of his neck.

"Clay?"

He looked over at her, then where she pointed.

A crudely written note instructed them to put down their flashlights, empty their pockets and the backpack onto the rock floor in the stationary beams of light. They were to open the bag of jewels so they could be seen from above, then put everything back and continue into the cave.

"Do as he says." He laid his flashlight next to Josie's and pulled out his pockets, then dumped the backpack contents to the floor.

He couldn't see Odell. He wasn't even sure Odell was up there, on the trail they'd been on just moments before, now looking down at them from the darkness. It made his skin crawl, though. The man had always been on the edge. From what Clay had seen so far, he'd say Odell had now gone off the deep end. He'd progressed from theft to kidnapping and murder. That was one hell of a leap, even for a man who'd faked his own death.

After a moment, he picked up the items from the floor, put them again into the backpack, including Ivy's teddy bear. As he scooped up his flashlight from the floor, he saw Josie's face. The look in her eyes gave him hope. All her maternal instincts burned in her gaze. She was like a mama lion going after her cub.

Not that he would have blamed her if she fell apart, but he was damned glad she hadn't and he was counting on her to hold it together. For their daughter's sake.

He couldn't let himself think of Ivy as they dropped deeper and deeper into the mountain, the air becoming colder and wetter. Bats scurried in front of them, a restless, frantic sound that set his nerves on end.

Water dripped and ran down the sides of the stone walls. Deeper and deeper. The narrow passages opened into rooms filled with rock formations. Rock sculpted by water and time.

He retraced the map in his head. Pit. Garden. Waterfall. End. Paradise. Points of interest? Except for End.

He shone the flashlight across the rock formations, standing like sentries. If he was right, this was the Garden. He hurried along the rock path worn slick by the feet of thousands of sightseers. If he was right, the waterfall would be in the next room.

But when he reached it, there was no running water. He glanced over at Josie. She pointed with her flashlight at a wall of brown flowstone that rippled and ran downward. ''The waterfall,'' she whispered.

He nodded and gave her what he hoped was a reassuring smile. She reached for his hand, squeezed it, then quickly let go as she pointed her light into the darkness ahead.

They dropped down a tight, steep stairway carved in the rocks and into a huge room filled with boulders. The air seemed denser. Colder. He shone his flashlight beam across the expanse.

Eyes. His hand with the flashlight jerked. Slowly, his hand shaking, he scanned the light back across.

The figure sat against one of the stalagmites. For just that split second, Clay thought it was Odell. Then he heard Josie gasp, "Mildred!"

She was tied to the rock formation, gagged and bound. Blinded by their lights, her eyes widened with fear.

"It's us," Clay whispered as he climbed up to her. He kept his eye out for Odell as Josie removed the gag and untied her hands and feet.

"He's got the baby," Mildred cried. "He's got Ivy."

"Do you know where?" Josie asked.

She shook her head. "He left me here and took the baby."

"It's all right," Clay assured her in a whisper. "Did you see where he went, which way?"

She shook her head, and he realized she'd been sitting here in the dark long enough that she'd become temporarily blind and disoriented.

He knew he couldn't leave her here alone. Nor would it make sense to take her with them. He also knew that Odell had anticipated this.

"Josie, give her your flashlight." Isn't that what Odell had planned for the second flashlight? "Mildred, I want you to follow the trail back the way we just came. It will lead you out of here. You mustn't be afraid.''

She nodded, looking scared, but tougher than most women her age. ''You're going to get him?''

Clay nodded. Or die trying. ''When you get out, go to my truck, lock yourself inside and wait for us. The keys are in the truck.''

''You want me to go for help?''

''No, that might jeopardize Ivy's life,'' he said.

She nodded, tears filling her eyes. She took the flashlight and the keys. ''I'll wait for you.''

He waited until Mildred disappeared back through the cavern, then he looked over at Josie. Her jaw was set, her eyes dark and narrowed.

''Ready?'' he whispered.

She nodded.

''I just want you to know,'' he whispered, ''you did the right thing with Ivy.'' There was so much more he wanted to say to her, but he told himself there'd be time after they got Ivy back. After Odell really *was* dead and gone. This time for good.

''Thank you,'' she whispered, and on impulse he leaned down to kiss her lips one last time before they got their daughter.

JOSIE FOLLOWED CLAY, her gaze on the small puddle of light that shone on the rock floor from his flashlight. The cave narrowed quickly, until she had to sit down and slide down a chute, the rocks overhead close and confining, cold to the touch.

Then the rock opened again. Clay flicked the light over a small room filled with stone statues huddled in thick clusters like lawn ornaments.

She knew they had to be getting close to the *X* on the map, which marked End. If they were right—

Off to her left, a faint light flashed on in one of the rock clusters. She swung around and let out a cry as Odell appeared out of the blackness like a ghost.

She clutched at Clay's jacket, but she knew he'd seen him, too.

Odell stood among the tall, misshapen stone forms. The flashlight he held just under his chin shot eerie, pale light up over his stark features, making it appear that he'd just crawled from his grave.

"You bastard," Clay swore.

Odell laughed, the sound echoing through the cavern, and lowered the flashlight. He'd wanted to scare them and he'd succeeded.

"Put your flashlight down," he ordered, his flashlight in one hand and a gun in the other. He pointed the gun at Clay's chest, the flashlight beam at Clay's knees.

He waited until Clay obliged, although Clay left the light on. The beam cut across the rock floor to shine like a small spotlight on one of the rough rock walls.

Odell moved toward them, keeping the gun aimed at Clay's chest.

"Let me see the jewels," he ordered.

Clay shook his head. "Where is Ivy?"

Josie saw that Odell had changed in the past two years. He'd lost weight. His face was gaunt, his eyes more deep-set, his body rangier. If anything, he looked meaner. Crazier.

"Not until I see the jewels," he said.

Clay swung the backpack off one shoulder and pulled out the bag of jewels. He hefted it in his hands, keeping it out of Odell's reach.

"I hope you brought the other things I told you to," he said, then grinned, his dark eyes flashing with evil. "Of course you did. You want to see that baby of yours again, don't you, Josie?"

"How could you involve an innocent child in this?" she cried. For even Odell, this was despicable. "What have you done with her? Tell me where she is, Odell."

"Listen to you, woman. I don't think you realize who you're talking to. I'm not your boy Clay here." His eyes narrowed, his face twisting into an angry sneer. "You talk nice to me if you want to see that kid again."

"Ivy!" Josie called, the sound deafening in the

cave. "Ivy?" The frantic sound echoed, then died into silence. "Ivy!"

"Quit that damn yelling," Odell snapped. "She can't hear you. I gave her a little something to help her sleep. Don't worry, I asked a doctor. No matter what you think, I wouldn't hurt *her*. Unless, of course, you make me."

Odell snatched the bag of jewels from Clay's hand. The bag came open and several jewels clattered to the floor of the cave. Odell's flashlight beam dropped to them. "Wait a minute, these aren't—"

Josie didn't hear the rest. Hate as potent as jet fuel rocketed through her. She launched herself at Odell without words, without thought, without fear.

It happened in an instant.

Odell caught the movement out of the corner of his eye. Shock registered on his face; this wasn't the same easily intimidated woman he'd known in Texas.

He tried to swing the gun, to get it pointed at her before she hit him, but without any luck. She hit him hard, barreling into him, propelling him backward into the stalagmites.

He hit his arm on one. The gun clattered to the floor. She pounded at his chest, his face, his head. He caught hold of her, smacking her with the flashlight just as Clay lunged for him.

The blow from the flashlight sent her flying backward. She tripped over one of the stalagmites growing out of the floor and fell hard, banging her ankle as she went down, the pain piercing through her anger.

When she looked up, she saw Clay and Odell wrestling. The gun lay a few yards away, near Clay's flashlight. Trying to ignore the pain, she slid over to it.

She'd almost reached the gun when she heard a loud crack behind her. She turned in time to see Odell's hand holding the flashlight hit one of the stalactites. The light went out, throwing most of the room into darkness. Odell let out a curse.

In the shaft of light from Clay's flashlight on the floor, she scooped up the gun, then the flashlight.

As she turned with both the gun and the light, she saw Clay slam Odell against the rock wall, his hands on Odell's throat.

"Where is Ivy?" Clay demanded. When Odell didn't answer, he threw him against the wall again, eliciting a groan from Odell.

"Don't kill him," she cried, trying to get to her feet. Her ankle wouldn't take the weight. She slid toward them on her bottom, using her good foot to propel her.

The beam of her flashlight lit on Odell's bulging face. "Clay, don't kill him. He's the only one who knows where Ivy is."

He seemed to loosen his hold.

"Listen to her," Odell gasped. "If you kill me, you'll never find the kid."

Clay instantly tightened his fingers on Odell's throat. "But I'll have the satisfaction of killing you."

Odell's eyes bulged. He tore at Clay's hands around his neck to no avail.

"Where's Ivy?" Clay demanded again.

Odell's face twisted in panic.

"Last chance." Clay tightened his grip on the man's throat again.

Odell's eyes went wild. He tried to move his head, but Clay had him pressed against the wall.

"She's—" It came out a hiss.

Clay gave him a little more air.

Odell's gaze flicked off to his right. "In the hole—"

The gunshot ricocheted through the cave, deafening. Odell slumped against the wall. Another shot filled the room.

Josie swung the beam of the flashlight in the direction she thought the shot had come from, pointing the gun toward an exit on the other side of the room.

Something moved, then disappeared around the corner of the cave wall, but not before she'd seen another light.

"Turn off the flashlight!" Clay cried. "You're making yourself a target."

She snapped off the light, her heart thundering in her chest, as the darkness enveloped them. Who in God's name had shot Odell?

She felt Clay's hand on hers. He took the gun, then the flashlight. She heard him move away from her. He shone the flashlight around the room.

Empty. Except for the rock sculptures. And Odell's body on the floor, blood still pumping out of the wound in his chest.

She crawled over to him and took his face in her hands. A slight gasp escaped his lips.

"Where is my daughter? Don't you dare die without telling me. Do you hear me, you bastard?"

"It's too late, Josie," Clay said from behind her, anguish distorting his voice.

"No," she cried, and shook Odell's head in her hands.

His eyes fluttered open. She watched him try to focus.

"Where's Ivy?" she cried, her voice breaking. "Tell me, Odell. Tell me, damn you, or may you burn in hell."

He looked up at her as if he might actually see her. "Crawl." The word barely escaped his lips. "Crawl." His eyes closed, and she felt the weight of his head in her hands and knew he was gone.

"Josie?" Clay asked.

She let Odell's head drop back.

"Josie, we have to get out of here. The killer will be back. For the jewels. For us. Do you hear me?"

"I can't walk, Clay. It's my ankle. I think it's broken, but I'm not leaving without Ivy."

He shone the light on her ankle and let out a low curse. "I'll carry you, but we have to leave, Josie. You have to listen to me—"

She shook her head. "We couldn't move fast enough with you carrying me and you know it The killer would catch us. You have to go after him." She knew that's what he wanted to do. He was only suggesting they leave because he wanted to protect her.

"He might know where Ivy is," she whispered.

"I don't want to leave you."

She could hear the pain in his voice, see it in his face. "You have to, Clay. Otherwise, he'll come back. Like you said, he isn't going to leave without the jewels." Or without killing her and Clay as well.

She watched him look toward the darkness where the killer had disappeared, trying to make up his mind.

"Go, Clay. I'll be all right."

He looked at her, then got to his feet, the decision made. "I won't let him get past me to you. I'll have to take the flashlight, though, Josie. I'll leave you the candle and matches, but the candle won't last long. Use it only when you have to. Stay here. I'll be back for you.''

She looked up at him, tears filling her eyes. "I'll be here, Clay. Just come back. Then we'll find Ivy and get out of here."

He touched her cheek, his gaze locked on hers. "There's so much I should have said to you, Josie."

"There'll be time. When this is all over," she whispered, turning to kiss the palm of his hand.

He scooped up the jewels and put them back in the bag. Then he checked Odell's gun for ammunition, shoved it into the waistband of his jeans and, picking up the backpack, removed the candle and matches. "I'll be back," he said, pressing them into her hands.

She smiled up at him. "I'm counting on it."

Before the last of the light from his flashlight disappeared, she lit the candle with trembling fingers. It flickered, illuminating a small circle around her, reassuring her with its paltry light.

She blew it out and held both the matches and the candle in her hands as she scooted back against the cave wall, away from Odell. She stared into the darkness, seeing nothing, feeling only pain. Ivy. The horrible ache for her daughter suppressed even the pain in her ankle.

Crawl. Josie closed her eyes and tried not to

think about the darkness. It had a smell, a feel, a texture that closed in the moment the candle went out. She squeezed her eyes tighter shut. Don't waste the candle.

Crawl. She thought of Odell's words. He'd said Ivy was in a hole somewhere. Crawl. She felt a chill scuttle across her skin.

She opened her eyes. Tiny pinpoints of light danced in the darkness. She closed her eyes again, unable to face such blackness. End. That had been the word on the map. Circled in red. Not long after the waterfall.

Could this be where it was supposed to end? Could the hole where he'd hidden Ivy be in this room? That would be like Odell. In fact, she remembered seeing his gaze flick to a corner of the room when he mentioned Ivy.

Carefully, she cradled the candle in her lap and, holding the matches, struck one. The sudden flare of light blinded her for a moment. She thought she'd dropped the candle, but there it was in her lap.

She lit it. The tiny, insignificant light pooled around her. She pushed the matches into her front pocket, then cautiously got up on all fours again. The candle flickered and she knew it wouldn't take much movement for it to go out.

She tried to get her bearings. They'd entered this room from the right. She hadn't noticed a hole, but she couldn't be sure. What she was sure of, was Odell.

Where had they first seen him? He'd have been near the hole. Guarding his prize, his ransom.

It took everything in her not to cry out Ivy's name. But hadn't Odell said he'd given her something to sleep and that calling for her wouldn't do any good?

She didn't know why, but she actually believed he'd been telling the truth. She moved slowly, carefully, holding the candle as if life depended on it.

Moving to where she'd first seen Odell, she shone the light along the wall, looking for a space deep enough to hide a child in.

The hole, when she finally found it, was small, almost round, and appeared deep. The others she'd found had been too shallow. But this one— Her ankle was killing her. She almost welcomed the pain. It distracted her from her real pain as she lay down on her stomach and slid into the hole and began to crawl.

Was Ivy in here? He'd said she was in a hole. He'd said he'd given her something to sleep. He'd said crawl. But he might have been lying. He might have meant something entirely—

She caught the glint of a tiny odd-shaped object on the narrow tunnel floor. Using her one foot, she pushed herself toward it, holding the candle high.

"Don't go out now," she said to the flame. "Not now."

She stopped and looked down at the small button in the shape of a bear's head. Tears rushed her eyes, blinding her. Ivy had been wearing her favorite bear pajamas with teddy bear buttons.

The candle flickered. She looked down at it through her tears and blew out the flame. It was hard to wait until the wax cooled enough that she could put the candle back into her pocket. But she did, moving methodically, carefully, slowly in a darkness that seemed denser, closer, almost suffocating.

She didn't need light, she told herself. She would find her daughter. Closing her eyes, she felt ahead of her, pulling with her fingers, pushing with her one good foot, dragging the other one, the pain almost unbearable.

She turned a corner and had to stop, the pain in her ankle making her dizzy and sick to her stomach and close to blacking out. She laid her head on her arms and wept, afraid she was going into shock. The sobs finally subsided. She thought of Ivy and slowly lifted her head from her arms.

Just a little farther. She could go just a little farther. She had to.

Then she smelled it. Baby powder. The scent seemed to float to her, beckoning her.

Chapter Fourteen

Clay moved through the cave, keeping his light dim and low. His mind raced ahead of him. Who had shot Odell? And why? To keep him from telling them where Ivy was? Or something else?

He frowned, remembering something Odell had said when he'd seen the spilled jewels. "Wait a minute, these aren't—"

What had he been about to say?

Clay stopped, hidden from view behind a space in the rocks, and pulled out the bag of jewels. He'd never seen them before, only in a photograph that Williams had given him after they were stolen.

Shining his flashlight over the glittering mass, he saw with a start that some of them had broken when they'd dropped to the rock floor.

A sick feeling settled in his stomach as he took one of the larger diamonds and ran the sharp edge across the glass face of his flashlight.

Just as he'd suspected. Paste. His daughter had been kidnapped for a worthless bag of glass.

It took all his willpower not to throw the jewels against the wall. He stared down at them and sucked in his breath as his anger dimmed and realization dawned, blinding bright.

He let out a curse under his breath. It was finally starting to make sense. Odell faking his death. Raymond turning up after two years. The missing jewels. Raymond's calls to Texas.

He pushed the jewels back into the bag, then looked around for a place to hide them.

Then he moved forward, knowing now what was waiting for him. Who was waiting for him. And just how desperate the killer was.

Ahead he heard a sound. The scrape of a boot heel on rock. He clicked off his flashlight and froze. The air suddenly seemed colder. He almost thought he felt a breeze and sensed that the narrow tunnel he was in opened into a larger space just ahead.

He held his breath. Someone was in the next room. He felt it. Thought he could almost hear him breathing. Sense him waiting in expectation.

The killer had the advantage. He knew the landscape in the cave and he knew where Clay would appear.

The darkness had its own ominous feel to it. Just a cold denseness that made it feel alive. He could see where it wouldn't take long in this kind of total blackness to go crazy, to hear the dark begin to whisper things in your ear that would drive you mad.

He reached blindly into the open pocket of the backpack for Odell's flashlight. It was broken and didn't work, but he'd taken it for the batteries just in case he needed them.

He now carefully and quietly unscrewed the end of the flashlight, took out the batteries and stuffed them into his pocket, working as quickly as he could in the dark. Then he twisted the end back on the flashlight. It was still heavy enough to cause a clatter if he dropped it. Or threw it.

Then, making sure he was ready, he moved forward, knowing the killer was ready for him.

JOSIE HADN'T GONE but a few feet more in the narrow confines of the hole when she felt something soft. The edge of a baby blanket.

She held her breath as her hand closed over one small arm. Hurriedly her hand went to her daughter's face. She felt warm breath and heard the wonderful sleeping sounds the toddler made.

Her face streaming with tears, she dug out the candle and struck another match. The flame flared, shocking her to see that Ivy lay curled in a cocoon of blankets against a solid rock wall where the hole ended.

A wave of panic swept over her. She felt as if the walls were closing in on them and there wasn't enough air for them to breathe.

But the look on her baby's face calmed her some. She touched her hand to it again, cupping her precious cheek. Ivy stirred a little, sighing in her sleep.

In the light, Josie could see that Ivy lay on a makeshift thin wooden sled of sorts. That's how Odell had gotten her back in here. That meant it would be easier to drag her out.

She noticed something else. An indentation in the wall. If she were careful, she thought she might be small enough to get turned around so she wouldn't have to try to pull Ivy and herself out backward.

The pain in her ankle had intensified. She wasn't sure she could crawl backward. And she knew Clay would never hear her cries this deep in the rock.

She put the candle down, gauging how much wax was left. She had to hurry. Otherwise she would have to do this in the dark.

The maneuver of getting turned around spent all of her energy but she finally managed it. She lay pressed against the rock wall for a moment, watching her daughter in the flickering candlelight.

Then she gave Ivy a kiss, snugged the blankets around her so nothing could get scraped and blew out the candle. Carefully, she put it back into her pocket along with the matches. The first thing Josie wanted Ivy to see when she woke was her mother's face.

Then she began the arduous job of getting them both out. Fortunately, the sled beneath Ivy slid easily along the rock floor of the hole. And this time, Josie knew where she was going and she had her daughter with her.

She felt as though she could move mountains. Just let Clay come back, she prayed. *Just let him live. His daughter needs him. I need him.*

CLAY FELT THE DARKNESS seem to change around him and knew before his hand lost contact with the rock wall of the cave that he'd reached the next room.

He hung back, afraid the killer would suddenly shine a flashlight on him. He dug the batteries out of his pockets, waited for a long moment, then threw the empty flashlight as far and hard as he could.

The flashlight clattered off rock, echoing through the cavernous room. A light flashed on, just as he'd anticipated it would. Off to the left. Back in the stand of stalagmites.

Clay threw a battery at the light and was rewarded with an ''umph'' and a curse. The light flashed out.

"I want my daughter, Williams," he yelled into the huge room, then dropped to his hands and knees and moved quickly and quietly across the expanse of stone floor that he'd seen in the glow from the killer's flashlight, Odell's pistol still in his waistband.

He didn't want to kill the collector. Not until he got Brandon Williams to tell him where Ivy was.

A shot exploded in the room, the bullet ricocheting off the rocks, then another shot.

Clay stopped crawling across the floor to pull himself up behind one of the taller stalagmites he'd seen in the flash of light, the second battery in hand, his mind reviewing what he'd seen of the room, anticipating where Williams would go next.

He wasn't surprised when he heard a scuffling sound off to his right. He'd hoped to push the killer in that direction. Away from Josie and that part of the caverns.

He threw the battery in the direction the sound had come from. Another shot rattled through the room, echoing against the rocks and followed by an oath and a loud thud as the collector must have fallen over something, too afraid to turn on his flashlight again.

Then another shot. The bullet pinged far off to the left, a wild shot.

"Tell me where my daughter is and I won't kill

you,'' Clay yelled, scrambling quickly away the moment the words were out of his mouth.

Two shots followed, then the loud click that Clay had hoped for. The bastard had a six-shot revolver, the most popular weapon in the West. And he was out of bullets.

Clay snapped on his flashlight, counting on Williams's arrogance. It wouldn't even have crossed his mind that he might need another gun.

But he would have more bullets, only Clay had no intentions of giving him time to reload.

He caught the dark figure in his flashlight beam and charged him, like a linebacker dodging through the stone statues.

He could see the man digging desperately in his pocket, his gaze blinded by the light. At the last moment, Williams heaved the pistol at him and tried to turn and run.

Clay ducked the airborne weapon and tackled the man. They went down hard. He heard the man's head hit the solid rock floor with a crack, then Clay was on him.

It only took a moment to realize that the man wasn't fighting him, wasn't moving at all.

Clay swore as he groped on the floor for the flashlight. It had rolled over against one of the rock formations, the beam shooting across the room to the tip of a stalactite hanging almost to the floor.

He grabbed the flashlight and swung the beam

to the soft, frightened features of Williams's face. But the collector stared up at him with a blankness that sent his heart into overdrive. Williams was still alive, but the fall and the knock on the head hadn't done him any good.

"The jewels," Williams whispered.

"I don't give a damn about your jewels. Where is my daughter?"

"I don't know anything about your daughter," he whimpered.

Clay felt panic surge through him. "No, damn you. You have to have some idea."

"Odell. That was his doing. All his doing. I just wanted my jewels."

"And I'd have gotten them for you, just like I said I would. You didn't have to kill Odell. You didn't have to try to kill me. Or—" He almost said "My family."

"Please, you have to get me medical attention," Williams whined. "I'm in terrible pain."

"Aren't we all," Clay snapped. He didn't know why but he believed Williams didn't know where Ivy was. All the man had cared about was his jewels and keeping his secret safe.

"You hired Odell and Raymond to steal them for the insurance money…only, let me guess, they got greedy. You risked my daughter's life for nothing!"

"Nothing?" Williams cried. "What about my reputation?"

"Your reputation is in the toilet and you're on your way to prison," Clay said, pushing to his feet.

He picked up Williams's flashlight. The man wasn't going anywhere. Not hurt and in the dark.

"You aren't going to just leave me here?" the collector cried.

"You're damned lucky I don't kill you."

Clay turned, his only thought to get back to Josie, get help. Medical help for her. Rescuers for Ivy. Then they would comb the caverns. The guides would know all the secret hiding places in the caves. He would search every inch of it. They'd find Ivy. They had to.

He almost ran back through the caverns toward where he'd left Josie, a promise on his lips to make everything up to her. First by finding their daughter.

He hadn't gone far when he thought he heard voices. The sound sent a chill through him. His heart pounded harder. He had to be imagining it.

He slowed, suddenly afraid that he might be losing his mind. As he neared the room where he'd left Josie, he saw the flicker of light. The candle he'd left her. He thought she must have been talking to herself. She sat huddled in a corner, the candlelight flickering on her body. Then he saw that she held Ivy in her lap.

They both looked up, their faces glowing in the light, as he stumbled to them. He could barely breathe around the lump in his throat. Or see, his eyes so blurred with tears. How? Where?

He fell to his knees beside them, his heart bursting.

"You found her." It was all he could say as he wrapped his arms around them both and burrowed his face into them, overcome with emotion.

He felt Josie's hand on his face.

"It's all right," she whispered. "Everything is all right now."

"I have to go get help," he said after a few minutes. He didn't want to let them go. Ever.

"Ivy and I will be fine."

The candle had almost burned out. He handed her the flashlight he'd taken from Williams. "I'll be back as soon as I make the call."

She smiled up at him. "I'm counting on you."

Chapter Fifteen

It had to be the longest night of his life.

From his cell phone in the truck, he called for an ambulance and the sheriff. Mildred stayed to meet the rescue team when they arrived and Clay went back to wait with Josie and Ivy.

When they'd finally gotten out of the caverns, he had ridden in the ambulance with Ivy and Josie, while Mildred drove his truck to the hospital to meet them.

In a separate ambulance, the sheriff had taken Brandon Williams. The coroner would take care of Odell. This time he would stay dead.

By the time they reached the hospital, Josie's ankle was swollen and she was drifting in and out of consciousness with the pain medication the EMTs had given her. Ivy seemed fine after her ordeal, her eyes bright with excitement. Whatever Odell had given her seemed to have worn off.

Clay counted his blessings while he waited for

the doctors in the emergency room to set Josie's ankle. Ivy had checked out fine. She'd only been given a mild sedative.

Just as the sun was coming up over the Bridger Mountains, Ruth joined him in the emergency room waiting room.

"How are you holding up?" she asked.

He'd had a lot of time to think. About the past. And the future. It was the future that he'd thought about the most while he'd waited.

"Fine," he said, giving her a smile. "Now that I know Ivy and Josie are all right."

She nodded. "You and Josie did great. Mildred told me all about it."

He didn't want to think about how it could have turned out.

"You have a beautiful daughter."

He glanced over at her in surprise, then realized Mildred must have told her.

She laughed. "Only a fool couldn't see that Ivy is yours."

"Yeah, well you're looking at one."

"You're too hard on yourself. You and Josie have that in common. I was hoping Josie would learn something from the horses. You don't force a horse. Maybe it's a lesson even a man as stubborn and narrow-minded as you can learn."

He laughed. "You don't think it's too late for me?"

"Not if you stop acting like a damned fool."

He heard Ivy's sweet laughter and looked up to see Mildred coming toward her with his daughter. Mildred had taken her down to the cafeteria for breakfast. Pancakes, Ivy's favorite.

Behind them, Josie limped toward him on crutches, her foot and ankle in a large white cast. She smiled at him, and he thought he'd never seen anything more beautiful.

"RUTH IS THROWING US a little party at the ranch later," Josie said, and looked at Clay, not sure of his plans.

"I'd love to go," he said. "You and I have to stop by the sheriff's office first. He needs a statement from us both."

"Mildred and I will take Ivy on home," Ruth offered. "The sheriff's office is no place for her, and I'd imagine you two have things to talk about."

"Subtle, isn't she?" Josie said after Clay had helped her into his truck.

"She's right, though. We *do* have to talk." He pulled out of the hospital parking lot and headed downtown toward the Law and Justice Center.

She braced herself, afraid of what he was going to say. Her heart didn't dare hope they could work something out with Ivy. At one time she'd feared Clay, as angry as he'd been, would try to take Ivy from her. After what they'd been through, she knew he wouldn't do that.

"There's something I need to say to you," he began. "I'm sorry. I was wrong about so many things."

"You don't have to apologize—"

"Yes, I do. I was afraid of getting involved with you and I suppose it was my clumsy way of keeping my distance from you. But I still got involved with you, anyway. I'm sorry."

She said nothing. He was sorry he'd gotten involved with her. Isn't that what she'd thought all along?

He must have seen her hurt expression. "Heck, Josie, what I'm trying to say is I'm sorry for the past. If I'd just faced my feelings for you none of this would have happened. But I'm not going to let another day go by without telling you how I feel. Not even another minute." He pulled over to the side of the road. "Josie, I want to marry you. I want us to be a family."

She let the words sink in. How long had she waited for this? So why wasn't she jumping up and down? Why wasn't she throwing herself into his arms? She'd trusted Clay with her life—and Ivy's. Why couldn't she trust this?

"I know you love your daughter," she began, but he cut her off.

"You think I want to marry you because of Ivy,

so I don't lose my daughter?'' He obviously could see that was what was bothering her.

''Josie, this has nothing to do with Ivy. I've thought of little else but you for the past two years. I looked for you in every face I passed on the street. I—'' He stopped and shook his head. ''Oh, hell.'' He slid over and, taking her in his arms, kissed her.

''Oh, Clay,'' she said when their lips parted. She knew she was holding back, but she couldn't help herself. There was still a lot they hadn't resolved.

IT DIDN'T TAKE LONG to give their statements to the sheriff. Brandon Williams had spilled his guts, hoping for a reduced sentence. Just as Clay had suspected, Williams had sold off all of the real jewels separately and replaced them with glass. The jewelry show at his gallery had just been staged to set up the robbery and collect the insurance money.

But Odell and Raymond, probably more Odell than Raymond, had gotten greedy and decided to keep the jewels for themselves. Odell had hidden them in Josie's great-grandmother's antique rodeo saddle just in case anything went wrong.

Things had definitely gone wrong when Josie took off with the saddle. But Odell had also underestimated Williams, not realizing just how desperate the jewel collector was. Williams had hired an unsavory acquaintance of Odell's to kill both Odell and Raymond.

Raymond had gotten away. Odell had gotten the better of the hitman, someone he'd done business with before in stolen goods. That had made it fairly easy for Odell to steal and switch their dental records and then stage his death, using the thug's body, complete with Odell's class ring.

It would have worked. But Odell couldn't stand the thought that Josie had the jewels in her saddle. Or that she had Clay's baby. The two things ate at him until he found her. But he'd wanted Clay, too, in his revenge scheme, so he'd had Raymond lead Clay to Josie and the jewels with an anonymous tip.

It seemed that Raymond had gotten squeamish, though, when he'd realized Odell planned to kidnap Ivy. Or maybe he'd hoped to get rid of Odell and keep the jewels for himself. Whatever his logic, that seems to be when he'd made the three calls to Texas, to tell them that Odell was alive.

He'd been too afraid of Odell to do more, the sheriff speculated. He'd probably also been worried that Odell would try to cut him out of his share.

Whatever his reasoning, he'd underestimated Odell. Odell didn't even wait until they had the jewels. He got rid of Raymond the minute he didn't need him anymore, following him back from the Toston bar to his motel to kill him.

Williams had trailed Clay and Raymond to Three Forks. He had to get those jewels before Odell tried to sell them. Or before Clay got his hands on them. The last thing Williams wanted was anyone to find out that they weren't real.

"Williams was broke," the sheriff told them. "He'd sold off the real jewels for cash to keep up his life-style. They were his to sell. Too bad he didn't stop right there. But he got greedy. Says he had a reputation to uphold." The sheriff shook his head. "Guess he didn't think he'd get caught. Imagine how a fellow with his demeanor is going to do in prison."

Clay could imagine, but he felt no sympathy for Brandon Williams. Or for Odell.

On the way back to the ranch, Clay put the past behind him and thought only of Josie and Ivy. He wanted them both at the Valle Verde Ranch, under his roof. He wanted Josie in his bed. What did he need to do to convince her?

THE PARTY RUTH AND MILDRED threw was nothing short of amazing, considering how little time they'd had to prepare. Josie sat with her leg propped up on pillows, watching the festivities whirl around her. Many of the neighbors had come along with people whose horses Josie had trained.

Ivy was decked out in her party dress, her eyes bright and shiny. Josie had to fight the urge to hold on to her, to wrap her in her arms and never let go.

Ivy was safe. Finally. She had to trust in that.

It would be hard to leave here. Hard to leave Ruth and Mildred, but she'd already extended invitations to them to come to Texas and both had accepted. Mildred had asked if she could bring Charley. It seemed that relationship had blossomed. Josie couldn't have been happier for her.

So much had happened. She felt overwhelmed. Clay wanted to marry her. Hadn't that always been her dream?

"You look like me," Ruth said, putting her cast next to Josie's. "Except you got a cooler cast. I can't hardly get any sympathy with this wimpy one." She lowered herself into the chair next to Josie, her laugh as warm and caring as her gaze. "Are you all right? Really?"

Josie nodded. "I have Ivy back."

"What about Clay?" she asked.

"He says he wants to marry me."

Ruth nodded. "Remember what I told you the first time you stepped into the pen? Don't let fear hold you back. Just figure the horses are as frightened as you are. Probably more. But if you show trust—"

Josie nodded, her eyes filling with tears. "You'll get it back."

Ruth smiled as she gave her a hug. "You've always been a quick study, Josie."

As Ruth released her, Josie looked up to see two pairs of dark brown eyes on her. Clay stood with Ivy in front of her.

"I want to be the first to sign your cast, if that's all right," Clay asked.

She nodded, her gaze locked with his. How could she deny this man anything?

"Ivy wants to be next," he said.

"She does?" Josie asked with a laugh, and noticed that they both had felt-tip pens in their hands.

Ruth excused herself to check on the food.

"I told Ivy that I didn't even think she knew how to write," Clay was saying. "She tells me I'm sadly mistaken."

He sat down next to Josie and, taking the cap off the pen, leaned over her cast. Ivy got close to watch him, anxious for her turn. Josie couldn't see what he was writing, her daughter's fair head was in the way.

Just having him this close warmed her, made her feel happy. She loved the smell of him, the feel of him, the nearness of him. And she loved the way he was with Ivy. Her heart cried out for her to give this man a chance.

When he'd finished, he uncapped Ivy's pen and

let her sign next to where he'd written. Josie watched her scribbles as Clay pretended to read "I love my mommy bigger than the sky, Ivy." He looked up at Josie with feigned surprise. "Not bad for a fourteen-month-old. I think our daughter is a genius. Must take after her mother."

Josie laughed. "I think she got her writing abilities from her father," she said, trying to see what he'd written. She looked down at the words neatly printed and large enough that she didn't have to bend close to see them.

Tears filled her eyes. Her heart swelled. She swallowed and read the words one more time to assure herself that she hadn't read even one of them wrong.

"I love you, Josie. Will you marry me?"

She raised her gaze to his and saw the expectant, hopeful look on his face. "Clay—" From the silence in the room, she knew everyone was looking at her, waiting.

"Just a minute," he interrupted. "Before you say anything, there is something else, something I didn't think should be said in felt-tip on a cast. Josie, I've never felt like this before. I don't just love you. I admire you. You're everything I've ever wanted and more. I want to spend the rest of my life with you." He stopped. "I'm crazy about you. I know you and Ivy don't need me, but I need you. I love you, Josie."

Tears filled her eyes. Those were the words she'd needed so desperately to hear. But it was the love she saw in his dark eyes that convinced her, love she knew she could trust.

She cupped his wonderful face in both of her hands. "You're wrong, Clay. We both need you. And love you."

The next thing she knew she was in his arms, his lips on hers. Very persuasive lips.

Clay pulled back to look into her face. "I want the three of us to go back to the Valle Verde and build a family. The sooner the better. You can train all of my horses. Please, Josie, say you'll marry me."

"Oh, yes, Clay," she whispered.

She could hear applause. She looked over Clay's shoulder and saw Ruth. Ruth had tears in her eyes as she gave Josie a thumbs-up.

Looking For More Romance?

Visit Romance.net

Look us up on-line at: http://www.romance.net

Check in daily for these and other exciting features:

Hot off the press

View all current titles, and purchase them on-line.

What do the stars have in store for you?

Horoscope

 **Hot deals**

Exclusive offers available only at Romance.net

Plus, don't miss our interactive quizzes, contests and bonus gifts.

PWEB

Coming in June from

Back by popular demand are
DEBBIE MACOMBER's

Hard Luck, Alaska, is a
town that needs women!
And the O'Halloran brothers
are just the fellows
to fly them in.

Starting in March 2000 this beloved series returns
in special 2-in-1 collector's editions:

MAIL-ORDER MARRIAGES, featuring
Brides for Brothers and *The Marriage Risk*
On sale March 2000

FAMILY MEN, featuring
Daddy's Little Helper and *Because of the Baby*
On sale July 2000

THE LAST TWO BACHELORS, featuring
Falling for Him and *Ending in Marriage*
On sale August 2000

Collect and enjoy each MIDNIGHT SONS story!

Available at your favorite retail outlet.

HARLEQUIN®
Makes any time special ™

Visit us at www.romance.net   PHMS